Divination and Deceit

Beth Dolgner

Divination and Deceit
Crones of a Feather Paranormal Cozy Mysteries, Book Two

© 2025 Beth Dolgner

Ebook ISBN-13: 978-1-958587-38-6
Print ISBN-13: 978-1-958587-39-3

Divination and Deceit is a work of fiction. Names, characters, places, and incidents either are the products of the author's imagination or are used fictitiously. Any resemblance to actual persons, living or dead, businesses, companies, events, or locales is entirely coincidental.

Published by Redglare Press

Cover Design: Melody Simmons

https://bethdolgner.com

contents

Chapter One   1

Chapter Two   11

Chapter Three   21

Chapter Four   29

Chapter Five   39

Chapter Six   47

Chapter Seven   55

Chapter Eight   63

Chapter Nine   71

Chapter Ten   79

Chapter Eleven   87

Chapter Twelve   97

Chapter Thirteen   105

Chapter Fourteen   111

Chapter Fifteen   121

Chapter Sixteen   129

Chapter Seventeen   137

Chapter Eighteen	145
Chapter Nineteen	153
Chapter Twenty	163
Chapter Twenty-One	169
Chapter Twenty-Two	179
Chapter Twenty-Three	189
Chapter Twenty-Four	197
Chapter Twenty-Five	205
Chapter Twenty-Six	213
Chapter Twenty-Seven	219
Chapter Twenty-Eight	227
A Note from the Author	231
Next in Series	233
Acknowledgments	235
Books by Beth Dolgner	237
About the Author	239

CHAPTER ONE

"I LIGHT THIS CANDLE..." Jo held the match to the white candle, but the flame sputtered and went out. She muttered something under her breath as she pulled out a new match.

"I'm pretty sure that word isn't in this spell, or any other," Valerian commented sardonically.

Marlee giggled, then forced the smile off her face. "Focus, ladies."

"I light this candle..." This time, the flame fizzled even before Jo had brought the match to the wick. She blew out a frustrated breath and pulled her coat closer around her body. "I can't do magic when I'm shivering."

"May I offer a suggestion?" I was cold, too, and I was looking forward to completing the spell so we could all go inside, where it was warm.

Warmer, anyway. The old heating system at the former funeral home was being repaired slowly. The radiators in our bedrooms were finally operating as they should be, but the living room and kitchen radiators were being stubborn. And, in early December in the Pacific Northwest, radiators on the fritz were not a good thing.

"I've got a fireplace lighter," I continued. "No matches needed, and no amount of shivering will make the flame go out."

Jo gave me a little smile. "Modern magic. Perfect."

The four of us were standing in a circle in the backyard, so I quickly dashed up onto the back porch and through the door that led into the kitchen. The lighter was in the junk drawer, and just a moment later, I re-emerged from the house, holding it over my head triumphantly.

Soon, Jo had successfully lit the candle, and she continued her part of the incantation. The candle was in the center of a folding table we had set up in the yard. We'd covered the table with a pretty blue shawl of Valerian's, and it was topped with all the items we needed for the optimism spell we were performing.

The sun had already disappeared below the horizon, and the last light of the day made the towering Douglas firs at the back of the property stand out in stark silhouette. The first stars were appearing above our heads, blinking out briefly as thin strips of cloud sped past.

"And I light this candle," Valerian said, beginning her portion of the spell. She lifted a purple candle and touched it to the white one Jo had lit. As she did so, though, her long, shimmering white hair swung forward, the ends coming dangerously close to the flame.

Instinctively, I jumped forward to intervene, inadvertently smacking the toe of my sneaker into a table leg. The table shook from the impact, and all four of us gasped in unison as the white candle teetered. Our sigh of relief when it settled back into place was breathed out as one, too.

We might not be the best at spell work, I thought, *but we are becoming a more coherent coven.*

And, ultimately, that was what counted. I had never been that great of a witch. My magical powers had always been average, but I knew the strength of a coven was about so much more than magic. The bond we created with each other was what really made us powerful.

Valerian held her hair in one hand, then leaned forward again to light her candle. Once she had finished her incantation, delivered in her strong, confident tone, it was my turn.

My once-blond hair—I still had scattered strands that weren't gray—was only long enough to brush my shoulders, so I wasn't worried about setting myself on fire as I stepped forward with my own purple candle. Marlee went next, and ten minutes later, we had completed the spell.

We wasted no time collecting the items we had used before we moved the table to the back porch, where it would stay dry when the expected rain arrived later that night. Even our familiars were eager to get inside. They had watched our spell from the roof of the detached garage in the backyard, then flown toward the open kitchen window the moment we finished.

Jo and Valerian led the way into the house, but Marlee held me back with a gentle hand on my arm. "Hazel, you've been making a lot of progress," she began. There was hesitation in her voice and sympathy in her brown eyes.

"But?" I prompted.

Marlee ran her other hand over her long black hair. The silky strands were pulled back in a low ponytail. "I can feel your hesitation. It's making me hesitant to even tell you that you're hesitant."

It was a strange statement, but it made total sense coming from Marlee, who was an empath. It was her strongest magical ability, and it served her well in her work as a wedding and event planner, but it could also be a hindrance to literally feel the emotions of others. I gave her a wry look. "I don't have enough money to fix more broken windows."

"Oh, you're unlikely to do that again."

I glanced in the direction of the small bathroom window, which currently had a thick piece of plastic sheeting taped over it. A month before, we had been working a spell for breaking down barriers, and I had broken something, all right. My magic had built up inside me, then ripped outward with enough force to crack the bathroom window right up the middle.

There was also a pane in one of the attic windows that needed to be fixed. At least my magic hadn't been responsible for that one. That was just normal old house—or, in my case, old funeral home—stuff.

"If only I could learn to fix things with my magical exhalations," I mused. "Just imagine: a great big cloud of pink magic swirling through the house, repairing every creaky floorboard on its way!"

"That would be a nice ability," Marlee agreed as we began to walk into the kitchen. "I could expel magic, and all the chairs for a wedding would set themselves up in perfect rows."

"And Val could pour ten beers at once, without lifting a finger!" I laughed at the image of Valerian behind the bar at Sit a Spell Tavern, pint glasses being filled by unseen hands.

"Why am I pouring ten beers?" Valerian asked. Marlee and I had reached the kitchen, where Valerian and Jo were already compiling things for dinner. These "Spells and Supper" evenings had become a weekly routine.

"Hazel was just saying she wished her exhalations could be controlled," Marlee explained.

"Oh, but the chaos is so much more fun." Jo winked at me with one of her dark-brown eyes.

After not practicing my magic for more than twenty years, I was slowly easing into witchcraft again. The magical exhalations—which I often thought of as magical farts because they were always unwanted and embarrassing—were inevitable as I learned to control my magic. It was definitely growing since I had returned to Foxfire Haven just four months before.

Thankfully, my coven had been nothing but patient and encouraging. The three women had moved into the old funeral home as renters, but we had quickly realized we were something more.

Something powerful.

Jo ripped open a bag of frozen peas and began to pour them into a pan. She straightened her shoulders and lifted her head while swaying her tall form gracefully. She spoke in a dramatic voice. "Would you ladies like to know your futures? The frozen peas will tell me all!"

The rest of us laughed. "Wouldn't it be great if you could divine your future and make dinner at the same time?" I asked.

"I've known some culinary witches who could do that," Valerian said.

"Talk about multitasking," Marlee commented as she grabbed a bulb of garlic.

"Jo, are the peas talking to you, or are they spelling out our fates there in the pan?" I joked.

Jo tossed her long black braids over her shoulder. As she did so, the purple streaks woven into some of them flashed. "You do know about Gemma Vale, right?"

"No."

Valerian made a scoffing noise. "Oh, she's full of it."

"Yeah," Marlee added, "full of peas."

I looked from Valerian to Marlee. "What are you two talking about?"

"Gemma Vale," Jo said, holding up a wooden spoon and waving it like a wand, "makes her living predicting the future by reading signs she sees in frozen peas."

I blinked at Jo. "You are kidding, right?"

Valerian gave me a skeptical look. "She's been around forever. I'm surprised you've never heard of Gemma, because I'm pretty sure she was already doing her pea scrying when you were growing up here."

"Foxfire Haven has always been a town full of characters," I said affably. "If I had heard of Gemma back then, I probably forgot about her because I was too distracted by people like Paula No-Pants."

Marlee burst out laughing. "You must be the one who's kidding now."

I shook my head. "Nope. I guess Paula moved out of town before you got here."

"More like moved on," Valerian quipped. "She died years ago."

"Anyway, she used to say she could only channel her magic if her legs were bare. I'd see her in the middle of the park, wearing nothing but a blouse and her undies, with her arms stretched toward the sky."

There was a loud caw from the direction of our familiars, and I looked over to see Lonnie, Valerian's raven, clicking her beak judgmentally. She was perched on the back of one of the chairs at the small table in the breakfast nook. Beside her, Jo's hulking pelican, Gordon, was bobbing his head up and down, as if he were nodding in agreement.

My familiar was tiny compared to Gordon. Burrowing owls were small, and Perkins was only eight inches tall, unless he stretched his legs out fully. He was perched on the back of another chair, his brown-and-cream head tilted affectionately toward Stella, who was Marlee's shy little toucan.

"Speaking of unusual witches," Marlee said, sidestepping Jo so she could put a pot of pasta sauce on the stovetop, "how did your last video call with Hailey go, Hazel?"

"She's as stubborn as I am." Witchcraft was passed down from generation to generation, but I had married a non-magical man. My daughter, Tara, hadn't inherited my magical genes.

Or so I had thought. Tara might not have been a witch, but she certainly carried witch DNA, because my granddaughter was one powerful little toddler. Shortly after her third birthday, she had let out a magical exhalation so strong it knocked over every piece of furniture in her preschool room.

It had also knocked over all of the other children. Thankfully, no one had been hurt. Since then, though,

I'd been coaching Hailey, both in person and through video chats.

"It's a shame Tara can't help," Jo said. "It's got to be frustrating for her to watch her daughter going through something she can't relate to."

"Yeah, she's scared," I said. I hated it for Tara, but I was doing the best I could to reassure her. "Hailey is too young to really understand what's going on, but it will get easier as she gets older."

Hopefully.

The worst-case scenario was that I would have to move back to San Francisco to keep a full-time eye on Hailey. A few months ago, I would have loved that idea. These days, though, I was happy being in the magical town of Foxfire Haven, Washington, again. I was even happy living in the funeral home I had inherited from Uncle Grant. It was full of life, now, and full of my friends.

Dinner was ready before long, and our birds followed us into the dining room, settling onto the makeshift perch we'd built for them using a fallen tree branch. We had a pleasant meal, talking about each of our days and how we thought that night's spell had gone.

After dinner, Marlee and I were loading the dishwasher while Jo wiped down the stove and Valerian got a pot of tea going. When Jo's phone rang, she pulled it from her pocket and frowned at the screen. "Why is my editor calling me after nine o'clock on a Friday night?"

"Newspaper emergency?" I suggested.

Jo answered the phone, then fell silent as she listened to whatever her editor was saying on the other end. Her look of curiosity quickly turned to one of concern, and she began to wind a finger around one of her braids. "Mm-hmm... Understood... Yes, of course."

After she ended the call, Jo looked around at the three of us. "I have to go back to the newspaper office. City Councilman Fortie Fortenbacher was just found dead in the middle of the park."

CHAPTER TWO

THE REST OF US gasped in unison.

"Dead? How?" Valerian asked.

"Was he killed? Right there in the park?" Marlee's eyes were wide. "I'm putting on a wedding there in two weeks. Ew. I'm going to go check the availability for other venues on that date." Marlee sailed out of the room, a worried look on her face.

"What kind of name is Fortie Fortenbacher?" I asked Jo. *Leave it to me to ask the important questions.*

"His real name is Allan," Jo explained. "Everyone in town calls—er, called—him Fortie. And I don't know any more than what I just told you. I'll have more details by the morning."

"Find out what he was wearing."

The three of us turned to see Holman, our resident ghost, shimmering in one corner of the kitchen. His light-gray suit was cut in the style of the nineteen thirties, complete with oversized shoulder pads, and his pencil mustache and wavy blond hair completed his retro look. "I hope for his sake it was something flattering."

"Why does it matter what he was wearing when he died?" I asked.

"Because ghosts wear what they died in," Holman said, gesturing at himself.

"Good thing you didn't die in stretched-out old sweatpants and a ratty T-shirt," I commented. Holman was notoriously judgmental about how people looked. As a former director at the funeral home, he was convinced his years of making the dead look good for funerals gave him the right to judge the fashion choices of the living.

Holman sniffed. "As if I'd own anything like that. Of course, a powerful death witch can change a ghost's clothing. It's a great way to get revenge on someone, because you can doom their ghost to have an unflattering silhouette forever!"

With that ominous pronouncement, Holman disappeared.

Marlee would be disappointed when she found out she had just missed the ghost. She had yet to meet him.

We wished Jo good luck as she hustled out of the kitchen. I was pretty sure I caught the same word she'd mumbled while trying to light her candle during the spell.

The news about the city councilman's death had cast a somber gloom over the kitchen, and Valerian and I finished our kitchen tasks in silence. Marlee returned while the tea was steeping. She was relieved there was an alternative wedding venue available in case her clients didn't want to marry in what she referred to as "the death park," but she, too, was downcast.

When I sat down at the kitchen table with Valerian and Marlee, we all stared at our steaming mugs of tea for a few moments before I said, "In a town this small, Fortie must have been well-known, since he was on the city council. I'm sure everyone in Foxfire Haven will be mourning his death."

"Don't be so sure." Valerian picked up her mug and blew gently onto the surface of the hot tea. "Fortie was a bit controversial."

"A bit?" Marlee shook her head. "You're being too kind."

"Then I'll be more blunt. Fortie Fortenbacher was one of the most pretentious men in Foxfire Haven."

Marlee laughed darkly. "And he loved to flaunt his power. If a business in town did something that made him unhappy, he'd threaten to use his status against them. The Salt Circle Cafe once made him mad, and he arranged a surprise food inspection. The inspector claimed someone called in a tip that the cafe had a rodent problem, and he shut it down during a busy lunch rush to do a thorough sweep of the place."

"That's a jerk move," I said.

Valerian nodded. "Which is why there might be a fair amount of people who will be happy to know Fortie is dead."

I was sitting at the table in the breakfast nook again the next morning, nursing a cup of coffee while stroking Perkins on the head, when Jo stumbled into the kitchen. "Coffee" was all she said.

"You sit down. I'll take care of it." I hopped up and got to work pouring a cup of coffee and adding three spoonfuls of sugar. How Jo could be so thin when she took so much sugar in her coffee was beyond me.

"I'm too old for this," Jo said as she slid into a chair. Gordon flew into the room and settled onto the back of the chair next to her, his giant wingspan threatening to topple a potted plant sitting on the nearby countertop. "There should be a law that when you're over fifty, you don't have to work past midnight, even for a breaking story."

"And with every year after fifty, you get to end your workday one hour earlier," I agreed as I set a mug down in front of Jo.

"And since I'm fifty-four, that would be four extra hours I wouldn't have to work. I love this idea. Let's find someone on the city council who's still alive and ask them to pass this law."

"What more did you learn during your long night?"

Jo shrugged slowly. "That Fortie was found face down in the middle of the park. That's it. I stayed at the office until two in the morning to learn nothing more than what we already knew. We'll have to wait on an autopsy to get details about what happened."

"So, there were no signs that someone killed him," I said. I watched as Perkins hopped from one foot to the other across the table, looking like he was playing a tiny game of hopscotch as he headed for Gordon. The pelican seemed to have become something of a big brother to Perkins.

"For all we know, Fortie simply had a heart attack." Jo shrugged. "Besides, who would have killed the guy?

He wasn't popular, but I can't imagine someone wanting him dead. I mean, sure, over the years I've heard plenty of business owners say they'd like to hex him, but it was always in jest. I think."

"You said he appears to have just dropped dead. Is there dark magic that can do that?" I remembered hearing rumors about it when I was growing up in Foxfire Haven. As a young teen, the idea of anyone possessing that kind of magical knowledge had seemed terrifying. Once I had gotten older, though, I began to think of those stories as nothing more than an urban legend. It was just something to scare ourselves with during a slumber party, and not something that really existed.

At the moment, though, I was reconsidering my skepticism.

"I'm sure there is dark magic that can kill someone immediately," Jo said. "In fact, I seem to remember learning about it in history class. There was a trial in one of the magical towns on the East Coast, back in the eighteen hundreds, when a witch was accused of making a farmer drop dead in his field."

"What was the outcome of the trial?"

"That part I don't remember." Jo looked thoughtful. "There are herbs, too, that could kill a person. I'll go have a talk with Adeline Beaumont later. She'll have some insight."

As the owner of the town's magical supply store, Adeline had a wealth of knowledge about herbs. She was also a vampire, and she was not my biggest fan, since she'd once caught me snooping around outside her store. Whenever I needed magical supplies, I shopped during the day, when there was no chance of running into her.

"I'm going to get showered and start my day," I said, rising. "I've got three deliveries to make, so it's going to be a busy one. Keep me posted if you learn anything more."

"At least Fortie didn't die in your garage," Jo said as I drifted out of the kitchen. "Have a good day."

Dead Easy Delivery only existed because the town's go-to delivery guy had been murdered in my backyard, and his body was found—by me—stashed underneath the old hearse in the detached garage.

I had needed income, and the businesses of Foxfire Haven had needed a delivery service, so these days, the black 1978 Cadillac hearse was hauling goods rather than bodies. It was a fun business that got me out of the house and helped me meet people around town.

The deliveries I'd been hired to make that morning were all fairly routine. In just three hours, I managed to get boxes of magical self-warming teacups moved from a storage warehouse to Stacey's Stationery and Sundries, and I took four dozen cupcakes from The Salt Circle to the nearby state park, where the rangers were celebrating a birthday.

The third delivery was scheduled for that afternoon, and it was a standard run for the Sit a Spell Tavern. I'd already made the drive between the tavern and the liquor distributor in the nearby town of Stanton so many times I could just about do it in my sleep.

With some downtime before that happened, I headed home for lunch and a halfhearted attempt at cleaning the hallways. Marlee was in the dining room, working on a spreadsheet for an upcoming wedding she was coordinating, and she would occasionally shout some words of encouragement from her spot at the table.

There were two hallways in the Taylor Brothers Funeral Home. The widest and grandest ran from the front door toward the back of the building, where it met in a T-junction with the back hallway. Double doors separated the two because the back of the building had been where Uncle Grant had his private living quarters. It was also where he had done his work; Jo's bedroom, which looked out over the backyard, had once been the embalming room.

I was vacuuming the worn but plush burgundy carpeting that ran the length of the front hall when I felt my energy sapping. Surely, I decided, it was a sign that it was time for a nap. First, though, I wanted to check the mail, so I walked out the front door and across the grass in the middle of the circular driveway.

Just as I reached the mailbox, I saw a blue sedan driving slowly down the street. The car slowed even more as it got closer to me.

I didn't need to see the driver, because I recognized Chief Constable Wyatt Hightower's car. What I didn't know was why he was pulling to a stop in front of me. Wyatt and I were neighbors, but we weren't exactly neighborly. He found me exasperating, at best, and I considered him to be the biggest grump I'd ever encountered.

The driver's-side window rolled down, and Wyatt's piercing blue eyes squinted up at me. Except, at the moment, they weren't very piercing at all. He looked exhausted, and his silver hair was tousled. "That wedding planner at home? I can never remember her name."

"Marlee Yamada. Yes, she's home." I nearly added a snarky, *Why, are you getting married?* but Wyatt looked too weary for sarcasm.

Wyatt and I had successfully avoided speaking to each other for about a month now, with the exception of the Foxfire Haven Samhain Festival, when we'd had no choice but to acknowledge each other's presence. We ran into each other every few days, it seemed, and there was one Thursday when I had run into him at three different places around town. Foxfire Haven was small, but it wasn't that small. We were usually polite enough to give each other a nod. One time, I almost got a smile from Wyatt.

Still, I was tempted to find a spell for avoiding someone.

Wyatt tilted his chin in the direction of the house. "May I?"

"Sure, go on in. She's in the dining room. Walk in, go straight, then turn right into the back hallway."

Wyatt pulled his car into the driveway, and he had already disappeared inside by the time I reached the front porch steps. I went into the kitchen and poured a cup of coffee, grateful Marlee had made a pot just after lunch. I had baked peanut butter cookies two days before, so I put three of those on a small plate.

What am I doing? I asked myself as I carried the coffee and cookies, plus sugar and a small jug of milk, to the dining room. *I'm supposed to dislike Wyatt.*

But he's exhausted, a little voice in my head answered. He had probably been up all night, dealing with Fortie's death, and despite Wyatt being the King of Curmud-geonly, I felt sorry for him.

After I delivered the coffee and cookies to the dining room, where Wyatt looked as surprised as I felt, I retreated to the living room. I was tempted to linger outside the dining room door so I could eavesdrop, but I didn't want to intrude on Marlee's privacy. Whatever she and Wyatt were discussing was between the two of them, I told myself firmly.

Though it didn't stop me from considering asking Holman to spy on the conversation.

Wyatt left about twenty minutes later, his tread heavy as he walked down the hallway. A moment after I heard the front door close, Marlee appeared in the doorway of the living room. She took a deep breath, then released it slowly, giving her shoulders and arms a shake as she did so. I wasn't surprised to see a bit of her dark-red magic sprinkle out of her fingertips and onto the floor.

"It's been years since I met Fortie," Marlee said, "so why did he have one of my business cards in his pocket when he died?"

CHAPTER THREE

"IF YOU DIDN'T REALLY know Fortie," I asked, "then why was he carrying around your business card?"

"It gets even more mysterious." Marlee plopped down onto the couch, then leaned her head back against the cushion and stared up at the ceiling. "Someone had written *birthday ritual* on the card."

"Is that a thing people around here do now?" Back when I'd been growing up in Foxfire Haven, we had thrown regular ol' birthday parties.

"No. I have no idea what that means. I help clients who are organizing big birthday celebrations, but the last time I checked, I don't offer any kind of rituals at my events."

"Why did Wyatt need to talk to you?" I was already perched anxiously on the edge of my chair, and I leaned forward. "Was it about your business card?"

Marlee waved a hand dismissively. "He says they're trying to put together a timeline for last night. Who saw Fortie last, and so on. He didn't think my card was significant, but he said when he saw you on his way home, he figured he may as well come in and ask me about it."

I let out a breath I didn't know I'd been holding, and I chided myself. There was no evidence Fortie had been murdered, and a business card wasn't enough to make Marlee a suspect. I was being silly.

"Maybe the constables will figure out who gave Fortie your card," I said, "and who wrote that bit about a birthday ritual on it. Maybe this is a good thing, Marlee. Now you know you've got someone recommending your services around town."

Marlee lifted her head and sat up a little straighter. "I hadn't thought of that. That's nice. Hopefully, in the future, that person recommends me to living people, who can actually pay for my services."

"What would a birthday ritual entail, anyway?" I touched a finger to the lines around my gray eyes. "Maybe it's a spell to keep you looking younger."

"Oh, that would be a great service to offer. I'd make loads of money adding something like that to my birthday-party planning."

Marlee and I were debating whether a birthday ritual to restore youthful skin would be more popular than one for less-creaky joints, when my phone rang.

It was Valerian, and she spoke loudly to be heard over the din at the Sit a Spell Tavern. "Hey, I'm on a quick break, and I just wanted to check in. The rumor mill is crazy! Everyone here has a theory about Fortie's death, and each one is more ridiculous than the last. Even Barry shared a theory, and he almost never talks!"

That last tidbit was a surprise. Barry the Bigfoot was a bit of a brooder, and ordering his preferred—and very expensive—single-malt whiskey was about the most Valerian ever got from him.

"Well, we were just graced with a visit from the chief constable," I said. Quickly, I filled Valerian in on Wyatt's chat with Marlee.

"Birthday ritual?" Valerian paused for a moment. "Interesting. I'll ask a few folks here what they might know about that. I'll keep you posted. Currently, half the patrons here are convinced Fortie isn't really dead. They think he staged everything so he can triumphantly arrive at his own funeral."

"Why would he do that?"

"So he can make a splash that will help him get re-elected next year." Judging by Valerian's tone, she was rolling her eyes and shaking her head.

Marlee got a good chuckle out of that theory after I filled her in, and she went back to work in the dining room, looking less shaken than she had following her talk with Wyatt.

I had brought an old shoebox into the living room with me, so I turned my attention to it. Jo had found it at the back of the highest shelf in her closet, where I hadn't spotted it while cleaning out the dusty embalming tools that had been in there when I first moved into the funeral home.

The shoebox was about half full of photos. Like the ones I had found in the glovebox of the hearse and the family time capsule buried in the backyard, most of the photos were of my uncle, Grant, and his friends. *The man must have had a camera on hand everywhere he went,* I thought. The ones in the shoebox showed an older version of Grant, which meant they must have been taken in the last decade or so before he died.

Uncle Grant kept popping up all over the funeral home in photographs, but he remained elusive. People in town had told me Grant had, as they put it, *gotten weird* in his final years. Even Barry had chimed in to say Grant had retreated from his friends, becoming secretive and mistrustful. Apparently, he'd been convinced there was something of value hidden either in the funeral home or on the grounds, and the search for it had become an obsession.

I really wished Grant's ghost was around so I could ask him about it to his spectral face.

I had to wake up far too early on Sunday morning. The weekend farmer's market was held at the park in the middle of downtown Foxfire Haven, and I'd been hired by one of the local farmers to deliver produce to a small restaurant they supplied on the outskirts of town. Susan, my client, had asked me to arrive at the park by 7:00 a.m. to beat the crowds, and while I was happy for the work, it wasn't going to stop me from grumbling about the early time.

It was a foggy morning, and as soon as I walked through the kitchen door, I turned right around and went back inside to add a scarf to my lightweight blue coat. It wasn't all that cold out, but it was damp.

I lumbered down my street in the black hearse, keeping my speed slow and peering through the fog. The street ended at the two-lane road that led straight through downtown Foxfire Haven. I turned right onto the road, and in just a few minutes, I was driving past the historic brick and wooden buildings of downtown.

Even in the foggy gloom, Foxfire Haven was a charming town. There were plenty of trees and flowerbeds along the sidewalks, and the park on one side of the street had a white gazebo and gorgeous green grass, even in December. Behind it, the Foxfire Haven City Hall rose dramatically, its white cupola obscured by the fog.

"Morning, Hazel," I heard as soon as I stepped out of the hearse. I turned to see two of the town's firemen walking past. They had been part of the crew that helped Marlee move into the funeral home.

"Hi, guys." I waved, enjoying the warm feel of the greeting. It had taken me a while to settle back into life in Foxfire Haven, and small-town moments like that were a nice reminder that I was acclimating.

The park was lined on two sides by white pop-up tents, where farmers were finishing setting out their produce. There was also, I saw, a local baker, and I had to stop myself from making a detour to buy a baguette.

"Excuse me," I heard a woman say in a crisp voice. "Hey, you, driving the hearse!"

I looked around and spotted a squat elderly woman seated under a tent at the very front of the park. The banner hanging behind her labeled the spot as an information booth for the market.

"Yes?" I asked, approaching warily. The woman looked like she was resisting the urge to hex me.

"You can't park there."

I looked over my shoulder at the hearse. I was parked on the curb, like the handful of other cars nearby. "Why not?"

"Because," the woman said, crossing her arms and peering at me with sharp hazel eyes, "everyone will think it's in bad taste after what happened."

The firemen had lifted my mood, and this woman was threatening to bring it crashing back down. I turned my head away slightly, trying to think of a polite response. That was when I spotted the inevitable memorial to Fortie. To the right of the tent was a pile of flowers surrounded by seven-day candles, photographs, and a few signs covered with phrases like *Always in our hearts* and *Gone but not forgotten*.

Apparently, not everyone in town had disliked Fortie.

I pointed to the memorial as I brought my gaze back to the woman. "I think the hearse fits right in." Her eyes flashed at that, but before she could retort, I scooted away. Behind me, I heard her spitting out words, though she was soon drowned out by the sound of early shoppers around me.

Susan's booth was in the center of one row, with a bright-green sign that read *Hothouse Magic*. I stepped up to her table, which was covered with cardboard boxes containing a broad mix of vegetables. A woman who looked like she was about eighty years old was already standing in front of the table, one gnarled hand gripped tightly around a black cane.

"I knew Fortie was going to die!" the woman with the cane said, nearly shouting at the woman behind the table, whom I assumed was Susan. She had a look of polite patience on her face as the old woman continued, "I knew he was going to die, and so did he."

CHapTer Four

I WAS SO SURPRISED by the woman's statement that I blurted, "How could you have possibly known Fortie was going to die?"

The woman turned to me, a smug smile on her face. "Because I know things. The peas have been telling me for the past six months that Fortie was at death's door! This lady here wants to sell you fresh peas, but frozen is the way to go. They'll tell you your future!"

I had to bite my lip to keep myself from laughing, and I twisted my face into what I hoped was a friendly smile. "I've heard of you! You're Gemma, right? I'm sure divining the future with frozen peas isn't something just anyone can do, so it really doesn't matter whether I buy frozen or fresh."

Gemma nodded and patted her short white curls proudly. "It's true that I do have a special aptitude for the art. But it's like any magical undertaking: you have to practice. Plus, witches have skills in different areas. For me, it's frozen peas. For you, it might be broccoli or even garbanzo beans right out of the can."

Our conversation was quickly veering off track, so I asked, "How did the peas indicate Fortie's death?"

"I've been advising Fortie for the past seven years, you know," Gemma said proudly. "Six months ago, the peas began to indicate death. The shapes they make when I throw them on the floor is how I divine the future."

"What shape indicates death?" I asked. As silly as I found the entire concept of frozen-pea divination, I was also curious.

Gemma brought the tips of her thumb and fingers together, forming an oval shape. "One of the most common omens is a skull. The eye sockets must be prominent. Otherwise, it's just a blob of peas and doesn't carry any meaning at all."

I nodded solemnly. "I'll keep that in mind if I give the peas a go."

"Oh, just come to me for a reading. It will be much faster for you than trying to master an entirely new art. And remember, there's a discount if you bring your own peas!"

"I might just do that. Thank you."

Gemma moved off, planting her cane so firmly with every step that I wondered if the park would need fresh sod to fill in the holes. She only got as far as the next booth over, where I heard her declare loudly, "I knew Fortie was going to die!"

Susan snorted, a hand clamped over her mouth.

"Is she always like this?" I asked.

Once Susan had gotten her mirth under control, she dropped her hand and looked in Gemma's direction. "She's very proud of her ability, but this is a whole new level of bragging for her. I know I'm laughing, but it's really not something to joke about. Poor Fortie. I wonder what really happened?"

"I guess we'll have to wait for the constables to announce that after the autopsy. In the meantime, hi, I'm Hazel. You hired me to deliver some produce to a restaurant."

"Yes, of course!" Susan leaned over the table so she could look down the row in the direction of the street. "Oh, and there's the hearse. How fun!"

It was my turn to snort. "Tell that to the woman at the information booth. She said it was in bad taste to park the hearse there."

"Why? Just because Fortie died here? People die all over the place. It must have been Donna McClelland who was scolding you. I expect she didn't want to look at the hearse because it reminds her of her own immortality."

"Mortality," I corrected.

Susan shook her head. "I spoke correctly. Donna is half harpy, which means she's not going to die anytime in the near future. She's not immortal, but she's close to it. She's tired of being an old lady, so seeing the hearse is a reminder that her body won't be in one anytime soon."

"That has to be rough."

"Still, it's not an excuse to be rude to everyone in this town. Forget Donna, let's talk about vegetables." Susan pointed to a stack of boxes at the back of the booth. "Those are all going to the restaurant, and you can use my handcart to shuttle them to the hearse. Do you want help?"

Some early-morning shoppers had just walked up, so I assured Susan I could handle it myself. Before long, the boxes were safely inside the back of the hearse. When I returned to Susan's booth to drop off the handcart, I purposely averted my eyes as I passed the information tent. I didn't want to give Donna any reason to begin lecturing me again.

On my walk back to the hearse, though, I ran into someone I wanted to talk to even less than Donna.

Euphoria Lachlan stopped in front of me, her mauve tailored suit and voluminous chestnut hair making her look more like the CEO of a big company than the mayor of a small town. "That hearse you insist on driving all over this town is a real eyesore," she said in greeting.

"I own a delivery service," I reminded Euphoria. "The hearse is big enough to fit my customers' goods into."

"Why don't you buy a truck, like a normal delivery service? It would look more professional."

The only reason I had started Dead Easy Delivery in the first place was because I needed some cash, and taking on delivery work had seemed like a good way to get steady income. After all, Uncle Grant's hearse wasn't going to make me money just sitting in the dusty garage.

I considered pointing out that the hearse was a perk of my business rather than a detraction. Most of my clients got a kick out of such an unusual delivery vehicle, and they would often ask to take photos of their goods going into, or coming out of, the hearse.

Explaining any of that to Euphoria, though, would be pointless. She had bullied me when we were kids, and she was still trying to bully me now that I was fifty-three years old.

So, instead, I answered in a falsely polite voice, "I'll take your feedback under consideration. By the way, I'd like to offer my condolences. I'm sure you worked with Fortie a lot since he was on the city council."

Euphoria blinked rapidly and placed a hand to her heart. "Yes, it's such a loss for the city. We're all very upset."

There was zero sympathy in her voice, and her acting attempt was terrible.

Maybe she can't fake grief this early in the morning.

I stepped sideways so I could keep walking, but I found my way blocked by a broad chest wearing the gray shirt that denoted the Foxfire Haven Constables. The circle around the silver pentagram badge told me who it was without me needing to crane my neck up to see Wyatt's face.

"Chief Constable," I said. I took yet another step sideways, but Wyatt mirrored my movement, so he was still directly in front of me.

"I never said thank you for the coffee and cookies the other day," he said. "I was so tired that it slipped my mind."

I opened my mouth to respond, but I was so startled by the polite tone that nothing came out for a moment. "Oh. Um. You're welcome."

"Why was she feeding you cookies?" Euphoria asked. She was looking from Wyatt to me with one perfectly penciled eyebrow raised. "And did they taste like embalming fluid?"

"I was at the funeral home on constable business," Wyatt answered. His firm tone shut Euphoria down instantly. She pressed her lips together, like she was holding in a retort, then she made a noncommittal noise and strode away.

I grinned up at Wyatt. "Thanks."

"Was she giving you a hard time?"

"Apparently, she's offended by the hearse."

Wyatt's eyes lit up with amusement. "Keep up the good work." With that, he deftly moved around me and continued walking down the row of booths.

I stood, too surprised to move for a few moments. I wasn't sure what was more shocking to me: that Wyatt had gotten Euphoria to stop being rude, or that he had been so nice to me.

Maybe he's not a curmudgeon all the time.

That was a pleasant thought, and the whole strange encounter left me feeling buoyant. I felt so good, in fact, that as I passed the information booth, I gave the old almost-immortal woman there a genuine smile and wished her a good morning.

Donna just scowled in response, but I didn't take it personally.

The restaurant I was delivering the produce to was located about halfway between Foxfire Haven and Stanton, the non-magical town about half an hour away. The restaurant's location on the four-lane highway that ran along that part of the Washington coast made it popular with road-trippers, and I wasn't surprised to find the parking lot full.

I pulled around to the back, where the manager met me and instantly asked for a photo of herself unloading a box of carrots from the hearse. Afterward, I helped her get the boxes into the kitchen while she came up with taglines for a social media post. "*We're dying to serve you good food,*" she mused. "How about this? *It's your funeral if you don't eat here!*"

The manager was so thrilled with the unexpected marketing opportunity that she insisted on feeding me breakfast. There was one open stool at the counter-top, and in short order, I was seated with a steaming mug of coffee in front of me and a breakfast burrito on the way.

I had quickly learned that Dead Easy Delivery came with some perks. One of them was the hospitality offered by clients. Free meals and even bottles of wine were among the things I got in addition to payment.

When I got home, I had a full belly and a full heart. Despite the best efforts of Euphoria and Al-most-Immortal Donna—as I was thinking of her—I'd experienced more kindness than coldness that morning. I felt energized, so I channeled it into working on deep-cleaning the bathroom. With all four of us sharing the one shower in the house, it needed to be cleaned regularly.

Adding more showers to the funeral home was on my short list of renovations I wanted to make, but it was going to be expensive. I'd have to deliver a lot of loads before I'd be able to pay for that.

Currently, Valerian and Marlee had each claimed one of the bathrooms that had been used for funeral attendees, but neither one of those had a shower. Jo and I shared the bigger bathroom in the living suite at the back of the building. An old clawfoot tub dominated one end, the dinged-up shower pipe curving over it in a graceful arch.

Getting four women to work out a showering schedule was no easy task.

Valerian called me in the early afternoon. "Have you had lunch yet?" she asked.

"No. I had a big breakfast, so I wasn't hungry."

"Come down to the tavern, then. You can eat up the local gossip, and maybe a sandwich or something. Marlee's here, and Jo says she's going to head over shortly."

My stomach growled, and I clamped a hand over my stomach. "I could do with a sandwich and gossip. I'll be there shortly." And, since the sun was tentatively peeking out from the clouds, and the temperature was mild, I opted to walk. It wasn't far from the funeral home to downtown.

Sit a Spell Tavern was across the street from the park. The farmers market was wrapping up, and it looked like half the white tents had been taken down already. The tavern was an architectural anomaly in Foxfire Haven, since it was a squat half-timbered building with a slate roof. It looked like it belonged in a medieval English village rather than a Pacific Northwest town.

The tavern was nearly full when I walked inside, but Marlee was sitting at the bar that ran along the lefthand side of the space, and she had saved me a stool. "Jo says she's getting takeout, so she doesn't need a spot," Marlee explained as I settled beside her.

Two stools away from me, at the very end of the bar, sat Barry the Bigfoot. His honey-colored fur shimmered in the dim overhead lights as he gave himself a shake. He lifted his whiskey glass, drained it, then lumbered out of the bar.

"I'm not sure I'll ever get used to the sight of a Bigfoot hanging out in a tavern," I remarked.

I was halfway through an egg salad sandwich when Jo's head appeared between Marlee's and mine. "Hey. I can't stay long. How's it going?" Before either of us could answer, she said, "Hey, Val, can I get the same thing Hazel's having, but to go? Thanks!"

"You busy writing a story about Fortie?" I asked.

"I'm not doing a thing at the moment," Jo said. "But the coroner is working today, even though it's a Sunday, so we're all sitting around, waiting for an announcement. As soon as we have details about how Fortie died, I've got to spring into action."

"It's exciting having a journalist for a roommate," Marlee said. "We get the scoop before everyone else does."

Jo wasn't listening. She had stepped back and was turning in a slow circle. Her eyes darted around, like she was looking for someone. Finally, she gave a little shrug. "Yeah. Wait. What did you say?"

"I said we always get the scoop from you. Who are you looking for?"

"Oh... No one. Just checking the place out."

Marlee and I exchanged a glance. Jo was definitely looking for someone, but neither one of us pressed. With a little sigh, she returned her attention to us. "I'm tired of this waiting around. As soon as I get back to my desk, I'm going to write an intention for news."

Jo's magical talent was in manifesting. What she wrote down with intention would turn into reality, though it often backfired on her in unexpected ways. Still, she was sometimes willing to take the risk.

No sooner had Jo left, a takeout bag dangling from one hand, than a man named Roscoe swaggered into the tavern. As soon as the door had shut behind him, he crossed his arms and lifted his head proudly. "Did you hear?" he said loudly, drawing the attention of everyone in the tavern. "The constables just announced Fortie was murdered, and there was nothing magical about it."

Chapter Five

My first thought wasn't about Fortie but Jo. She had only talked about writing an intention, but had she still managed to work some manifesting magic? My second thought was about the tail end of Roscoe's announcement. If he knew Fortie hadn't been killed through magical means, then that meant he also knew how Fortie had met his demise.

Marlee and I had both swiveled around on our stools to gaze at Roscoe, and behind me, I heard Valerian make a noise of disbelief. "Murder?"

Roscoe took a few more steps forward, until he was standing directly in the center of the tavern. He was clearly enjoying being the center of attention, and even amid my shock over the news that Fortie had been murdered, I still felt a surge of annoyance. Roscoe had been close friends with Uncle Grant for decades. But, when Grant had begun to act erratically in his later years, Roscoe had abandoned him. These days, his snide remarks about Grant would never give someone the impression the two of them had once been good friends.

And, because Roscoe had so much contempt for Grant, that sentiment extended to Grant's family members, too. Roscoe and I weren't going to be best buds anytime soon, and we tended to steer clear of each other anytime we were both at the tavern.

"Everyone knows Fortie was found face down in the middle of the park," Roscoe began, still speaking loudly. "It looked like he had simply dropped dead, probably of natural causes. A heart attack, or some other medical condition that could hit"—Roscoe snapped his fingers—"at any moment."

"Oh, get to the point," Valerian muttered. I glanced over my shoulder to see her leaning on the bar, her chin propped in her hands.

"Our constables, of course, took the matter very seriously," Roscoe continued. "After all, a prominent member of Foxfire Haven society—a city council member, no less—had just died, right in the middle of a public park."

I was with Valerian: Roscoe was taking entirely too long to tell his story. I was beginning to feel agitated because I was so eager to know how, exactly, Fortie had been murdered, but Roscoe was dragging things out to enhance the drama.

As I got more impatient and more agitated, I could feel my magic beginning to build up. *No, no, no,* I thought, trying to will my magic to settle down. That, in turn, only made me more frustrated and impatient, which further increased my magic.

I knew how this would end if I didn't do something soon. I would no longer be able to hold in all the magic that was building up inside me, and it would explode out of my body with force.

Slowly, in an effort to not draw attention to myself, I slid my hand onto the bar. A moment later, I felt Valerian's hand over mine. She chanted something too low for me to hear, just as she had done once before when my magic had been on the verge of erupting from me.

Marlee glanced over at me with a sympathetic look, and I knew she was feeling my frustration and fear.

I focused on Valerian's soothing touch as I took a few deep breaths. When I finally felt confident enough to return my attention to Roscoe, I wasn't surprised to discover he was still droning on.

Eventually, though, he got to the point. "It was an injection." Roscoe stopped to look around, savoring everyone's rapt attention. "Extract of deadly nightshade. Someone probably walked right up to him and shoved a needle into his body. Fortie was dying before he'd even realized what was going on."

"How do you know all of this, Roscoe?" Valerian called. She sounded like she only half-believed him.

Roscoe sniffed and threw an annoyed look in our direction. "Eh, I have my sources."

Everyone in the tavern began discussing Roscoe's news, and Marlee and I turned back to the bar. Marlee was already pulling out her phone, and a moment later, she said, "Jo, Roscoe claims Fortie was murdered by some kind of injection. Is that true?"

After a few moments of silence, Marlee nodded. "Wild. Okay. Thanks." She ended the call and looked at me, since Valerian had moved off to serve a group farther down the bar. "Jo says the constables put out a statement, and it's exactly what Roscoe said."

"But who would have killed him?" I asked. "And why?"

Marlee groaned and rested her head in her hands. "And why did my business card have to be on him when it happened?"

I leaned over until my shoulder touched Marlee's. "Hey, don't worry. That doesn't make you a suspect."

"You're right. But it is a little unsettling. My business card just became evidence in a murder investigation."

Valerian had rejoined us as Marlee was talking, and she frowned in Roscoe's direction. "What's unsettling is that there's been another murder in our town. I don't like it. And I don't appreciate people like Roscoe taking such delight in it."

"Just don't tell him about my business card!" Marlee gave a weak laugh. "You're right, Haze, I shouldn't worry about it. In fact, I'm going to walk outside, shake off all this frustration of yours that I absorbed, and head to my storage unit to inventory wedding reception center-pieces."

The tavern had gotten more crowded shortly after the news of Fortie's murder, and I expected it was people who were eager to get together and gossip. Valerian was busy, but she would rake in the tips. I needed to get a few supplies at Into the Cauldron, the town's magical supply store, so I soon said goodbye to Valerian and headed out, too.

Into the Cauldron was a short walk from the tavern, and as I went, I tried to wiggle my hands and arms to help shake off some of that excess magic I'd built up during Roscoe's revelation.

The magic store was both comforting and alarming for me. Being around so many magical supply items, like herbs and crystals, raised my magic. Until I learned to have better control over it, I would continue to be nervous in any kind of situation that amped it up. At the same time, though, there was something delightful about wandering the narrow aisles of the store. The riot of smells from various herbs and incenses made the shop feel like a real departure from the world outside, and the cluttered shelves had a sort of homey feeling. It felt, I had decided during one of my visits, exactly like a magic store should: slightly chaotic but cozy at the same time.

The teenaged clerk who often worked during daylight hours was behind the counter when I brought the items I needed to the cash register. She looked bored, until she spotted the dried comfrey I'd put down on the counter. "You're doing a protection spell?" she asked, her eyes widening. "Do you think that guy's killer is going to come after you next?"

I laughed at how dramatic she sounded, but I shook my head. "No, comfrey can be used for control spells, too. That's what I need it for."

"Good, because I'm not sure it really protects, anyway. That dead city council guy used to buy this all the time."

I tilted my head. "Was Fortie buying it for protection?"

The teen shrugged. "He must have been, because he also stocked up on vervain, malachite, and mother-of-pearl. All of those have various uses, but they've only got one thing in common."

"They're used in protection magic or as wards against danger." Even though I had avoided witchcraft for twenty years, I still remembered the basics. "That would imply Fortie knew someone was after him."

Which means, I realized, *he knew the peas weren't just indicating death. They foresaw his murder.*

Had Gemma known? Had she also seen murder in Fortie's frozen peas, or had he been the one to make that assumption?

I was lost in thought long enough that the clerk cleared her throat and said pointedly, "So, um, cash or card for this stuff?" I looked down to realize she had already rung up all of my items and put them in a paper bag.

Even as I paid, I was still mulling over the clerk's comments about Fortie. If he had known someone disliked him enough to want him dead, then hopefully, the constables would find a trail leading to that person. "Good luck, Wyatt," I said under my breath as I left the store.

Before I began my walk home, I really needed to get rid of my excess magic. It hadn't built up too much inside the magic store, but between that and the tavern, I could tell I was right on the verge of a magical exhalation.

And I did not want to break another window.

I also didn't want to have another public display of my inability to control my magic. So, with that in mind, I ducked down a side street shortly after leaving the magic store. There was a recessed doorway that would be a perfect spot for doing a quick spell I'd learned for shedding excess magic.

I pulled the comfrey out of my shopping bag and held it tightly in my hand. I focused on the way it pressed against my palm, and I imagined power passing from it into my body. I murmured the words that went with the spell, and my body began to feel uncomfortably warm.

The first time I had performed the spell, I thought for sure I was having a hot flash. Eventually, I had realized it was just a part of the process.

The heat built up as I continued, and I felt a strange sensation all over my body, like unseen fingers tapping against my skin in unison. A pink cloud of magic puffed out around me, then slowly settled to the ground at my feet.

I breathed out a sigh of relief. The spell had worked, and I could head home without worrying about any incidents.

I lazily kicked at the lingering magic, trying to make it dissipate faster. As I did so, I heard voices coming from the sidewalk out on Main Street, just a few feet from where I was hidden.

There was no mistaking Euphoria's voice. "I asked Hightower to keep it quiet if it was confirmed as murder. This is the last thing we need to be dealing with."

A man's voice that I didn't recognize responded, "Haven't you realized Fortie's death is good for us? I hope they catch the killer soon, so we can send them a thank-you card."

CHAPTER SIX

I RISKED PEEKING OUT from the recessed doorway, and I was just in time to see Euphoria and the man passing from view. Since I only got a look at the backs of their heads, I had no idea who the man was.

But I did know I didn't like him. He had sounded almost happy about Fortie's murder.

Just before Euphoria and the man moved out of earshot, he added, "Foxfire Haven is better off without his type."

What type is that?

I remembered what my roommates had said about how Fortie had let his power and position go to his head. Maybe he had bullied the wrong business owner, and he had died because of it.

I didn't know if the snippet of conversation I had just overheard was relevant to the murder investigation, but after not disclosing every detail I'd learned back when the constables were trying to solve Steve Zillmann's murder, I had decided it would be better to pass along too much information rather than not enough.

I really hoped Wyatt wasn't working, because I would prefer to pass along a tip to a constable I didn't know rather than deal with his grumpiness.

There was still a bit of my pink magic around the bottom of the doorway where I was standing, so I stomped my feet in an effort to dissipate the last of it. Once I only saw a pale shimmer of pink in one corner, I decided that was good enough and headed out.

I looked in the direction Euphoria and the unknown man had been walking after I reached the sidewalk, but they were nowhere to be seen. They had either turned a corner or gone inside one of the businesses along Main Street. I considered looking for them but quickly decided against it. I didn't want them to know I had overheard them talking about Fortie, and the last thing I wanted at the moment was to be face-to-face with Euphoria again.

I only got half a block down Main Street, when the door of a restaurant called Foxfire Grill opened, and Wyatt stepped out onto the sidewalk.

Oh, great.

Wyatt was wearing his constable uniform—a gray shirt and a pair of black pants—which meant he was, after all, on duty. As I watched, he lifted a hamburger to his mouth and took a bite, leaning over to avoid dripping anything onto his uniform.

I was having an internal debate about whether to simply nod in acknowledgment of his presence or tell him about the overheard conversation. *I can continue on to the constable station and tell someone who's not on break, like Wyatt is,* I told myself.

That, of course, was just an excuse.

Just as I opened my mouth to say something, though, the pungent smell of horseradish and jalapeños hit my nostrils. "Oh!" I brought a hand up to my nose. "Ew."

Wyatt turned toward me at the sound of my voice, and his eyes bored into me as he slowly chewed and swallowed. Finally, he waved the burger in my direction. "Just because you don't like it doesn't mean it's not delicious."

"If you're going to interrogate a suspect after this, they'll confess in a heartbeat as long as you promise to stop breathing in the same room as them." My hand, which had been covering my nostrils, slid down a fraction to cover my mouth. I could be opinionated, sure, but it was rare for me to blurt out something that rude.

Wyatt gestured toward the empty sidewalk on either side of us. "If you hate the smell that bad, then what's stopping you from continuing on?"

"I need to tell you something."

"Is this about the magical exhalation you just had?" Wyatt glanced down at my feet and raised his eyebrows. I followed his gaze to see a bit of magic still clinging to the toe of my left sneaker.

I tapped the toe of my shoe against the sidewalk, trying to shake off the excess magic while chastising myself for not giving my shoes a thorough check after I'd left the doorway. "It was a controlled shed. No one got hurt."

Wyatt just grunted in response.

"Anyway," I said as Wyatt took a lazy bite of his burger, "I was on my way to the constable station to report something, so I may as well tell you now." I quickly described the conversation between Euphoria and the man, ending with, "I thought you might want to look into it."

"If the man said he and the mayor should be grateful to the killer, then that means they're not the killers themselves," Wyatt pointed out.

"Well..." I felt my shoulders droop. He had a point. "You're right."

"Lots of people in this town didn't care for Fortie, so I don't think what you overheard is all that surprising. You running to me with this information wouldn't have anything to do with your personal feelings toward the mayor, would it?"

"Why would the mayor ask you not to announce the news that Fortie's death was murder?" I countered.

"So people like you wouldn't panic and come up with wild accusations."

I resisted the urge to smack the half-eaten burger right out of Wyatt's hands. Instead, I said, "I have to go."

"You got a date or something?"

"I'm going to have a video call with my granddaughter." I stopped myself before adding that I was helping Hailey learn to control her magic. Wyatt, I knew, would scoff at the idea of me teaching anyone magical control.

I left Wyatt to his stinky burger and stalked past him, stewing the entire walk home. Wyatt and I really knew how to push each other's buttons, and it had all started because his cat had been bullying my familiar. I had to wonder, though, if anything would be different, even if we had met under pleasant circumstances. Wyatt was a bona fide grump.

My mood went from annoyed to cautious as I walked up my circular driveway toward the red-brick funeral home. The front door was standing wide open.

Again.

It had happened a few times before, and I had yet to find a good explanation for it. When I left for downtown, I had locked up behind me, and I trusted my roommates to do the same as they came and went.

I stopped on the front porch and called through the open doorway. "Hello?"

The long hallway that ran to the back of the house was dim, but after a moment, I could see a form moving toward me, its body draped in white.

As the form got closer, I relaxed. It was Marlee. She was wearing a bathrobe and towel-drying her hair as she approached. "Hi, Hazel. Did you call? I just got out of the shower."

"I got home and found the front door like this."

Marlee frowned. "I closed and locked it when I came home, like I always do."

I stepped over the threshold and shut the door. I engaged the deadbolt, then gave the door a tug. It didn't budge. The lock was working just fine, so the door shouldn't have been able to open.

"Maybe Holman did it?" Marlee asked.

"I've asked him on previous occasions, but he always says he didn't do it. The last time I brought it up, he suggested we must simply be forgetful old ladies." Having a snarky ghost in the funeral home resulted in a lot of bizarre conversations. "But, I'll ask him again."

Getting Holman to show up, though, wasn't as simple as calling his name. He only ever bothered to appear when he had something to critique, like an outfit or a hairstyle.

I grinned. "I'm off to put on a tacky outfit."

Marlee's face lit up. "Oh, what a great idea! However, as much as I want to meet Holman, I'd rather do it when I'm wearing more than a robe. Fill me in later on what you learn about the front door."

I promised to do just that before Marlee disappeared into her room. She was in one of the former chapels—there was one on either side of the hallway—which was complete with stained-glass windows.

My room was farther back, just off the kitchen and dining room in the private living suite. It was smaller and far less pretty than Marlee's and Valerian's chapel rooms, but I liked how cozy it felt.

I headed for my closet and picked out the worst outfit I could assemble: a silky purple floral top and a long winter skirt in a blue-and-green plaid. I put my sneakers back on and even added a bright-yellow necklace for good measure.

When Holman didn't instantly show up to comment on my outfit, I shrugged and went into the kitchen to tidy up. I was halfway through unloading the dishwasher when I saw movement out of the corner of my eye. I looked over to see Holman standing there, his arms crossed as he shook his head slowly.

"Lady, what are you wearing?"

"Do you like it?" I twirled around, the skirt billowing out around my ankles.

"Of course not. You don't have the best fashion sense, but you're smarter than this." Holman paused, then gasped. "You did this on purpose because you need to talk to me."

"Guilty as charged," I admitted. "The front door was wide open when I got home this afternoon. Marlee says it was closed and locked before she got in the shower. Did you open it?"

Holman shook his head again. "It hasn't been me any other time, and it wasn't me today. I can't manipulate physical objects. If I could, I would move a few items of clothing from Valerian's closet straight into the trash bin."

"I just don't understand why the door keeps opening. Do we have another ghostly roommate who's doing it?"

"Not that I'm aware of." Holman looked thoughtful. "I do remember the door opening once or twice back before Grant banished me. That was ages ago, and nothing bad ever came of it then. I wouldn't worry about it."

"You're probably right. Thanks, Holman. I'm going to change back into my normal clothes now."

"I appreciate that." Holman gave me a wicked smile before he disappeared.

I got changed before settling in at the kitchen table, my cell phone propped on a stack of books so I could have a video call with Hailey. Tara, my daughter, called right on time, and after a quick catch-up with her, she moved out of the camera's view, and Hailey appeared.

"Gamma!" Hailey gave me a toothy smile, her dimples making her look even more adorable. "Magic time!"

"That's right, Hailey. We're going to keep playing the game we started last time. Do you remember how it goes? First, we sing a song about feeling our magic."

Hailey didn't seem interested at the moment, because she interrupted me. "Look, Gamma!"

Hailey stared intently at the camera, then the image of her flickered, and the screen went black.

CHAPTER SEVEN

I TAPPED THE SCREEN of my phone. It was still working, but the call had somehow disconnected.

My son-in-law's name popped up on the screen, alerting me that I was getting a video call from his phone. When I answered, though, I saw Tara rather than Brian. Her eyes were darting between the camera and something to one side—or, more likely, someone.

"What just happened?" Tara asked in a shaky voice.

"I was going to ask you the same thing! Hailey wasn't touching anything, but the call dropped." Of course she hadn't needed to touch the phone, I realized. She had probably ended the call with her magic.

"My phone is fried." Tara sighed. "I think Hailey zapped it."

Definitely magic, then.

I could hear Hailey giggling in the background as I gave Tara a sympathetic look. "It's normal for a young witch to cause a bit of electrical chaos."

I didn't add that while those incidents were common, they weren't usually intentional. Children learning to control their magic would accidentally fry a TV, computer, or any other electronic device that got tangled up with their magical energy.

Hailey, however, had seemed to fry the phone on purpose.

Tara was probably thinking along the same lines, because she sighed again. "I guess I'd better go check every appliance in the house. She's probably been practicing on other devices. I sure hope the microwave still works."

"Before you do that, let me talk to Hailey briefly. I want you to hear this, too."

Soon, I was looking at my granddaughter again. "Honey," I said gently but firmly, "do you remember that bedtime story about the good witch?"

Hailey nodded.

"The good witch only uses her magic to do nice things. She helps people, remember?"

"And the cat."

"That's right. She helped a boy get his cat out of a tree. I want you to only use your magic to do nice things, too. It's not nice to break your mom's phone, is it?"

"No." Hailey looked away. "Mama, I fix."

"That's okay, Hailey," I heard Tara say. "You don't need to fix it. But don't do it again."

"Kay."

We moved on with our lesson, but I felt unsettled even as Hailey worked on the game we'd created to help her recognize when her magic was growing so she could control it. She was shaping up to be a talented witch. As an adult, it would be great for her to have strong magical abilities. As a child, though, she was going to be a menace.

The call ended after Tara and I chose the day and time for Hailey's next lesson, and long after I said good-bye, I sat at the kitchen table with my head in my hands. Perkins had been watching the whole thing from his little nest by the radiator, and he half-flew, half-hopped across the table until he was pressed against my forearms. I slid my hand down and stroked his head.

Perkins leaned his face into my palm, nuzzling gently with his tiny beak. I could feel the calming energy radiating from him. It was amazing how such a little animal could be such a big help, and I smiled down at my familiar. "Thanks, Perky," I whispered.

Marlee stomped into the kitchen and stopped directly in front of the table as I lifted my head. She plucked at the cream-colored sweater she was wearing. "Do I look awful? I feel like everyone is going to look at me and think I'm boring. They'll say I'm just plain and forgettable, not interesting, like you and Val and Jo."

I stared, open-mouthed, at Marlee. Perkins seemed to be confused, too, because he tilted his head sideways and made a chirping noise that sounded like a question. "You look great," I finally said. "And you are definitely not boring."

Marlee stared at me so long I began to squirm in my chair. "It's not you," she said as she blinked and looked away. "Jo and Val are out, right?"

"Yes. You're thinking that you've picked up on someone else's feelings."

"Exactly. But if you're the only one home, and you're not feeling like you're forgettable and ordinary, then who is it coming from?"

I picked up my phone and waved it in the air. "I just got off a video call with Hailey, but she's definitely not feeling down. She gleefully fried Tara's phone with her magic."

"Oh." Marlee drew the word out. "Tara. I must be feeling your daughter's emotions, even though she's all the way down in San Francisco."

I shook my head. "Tara is frustrated and scared about what Hailey might accidentally do with her magic, but she's not moping around feeling like the boring one of the bunch."

"But she is," Marlee insisted. She slid into a chair at the table, and her familiar, who had been sharing the small nest with Perkins, fluttered over to sit on her shoulder. Stella lowered her head until the tip of her long yellow beak tapped Marlee's collarbone. It looked like a toucan's way of patting someone on the shoulder to give comfort.

"It must be hard for Tara," Marlee continued. "She's got a mom and a daughter who are both witches, but she's not magical at all."

"But Tara hated that I was a witch. Remember, I gave up my magic for twenty years because she was so embarrassed by my abilities."

"Of course she was embarrassed by it when she was growing up. She didn't want to be the kid with the weird mom. Those little girls at her sleepover who caught you working a spell are probably still telling stories about it! But I expect Tara felt some jealousy, too."

"If she did, she never articulated it."

"She might not realize how strongly she feels about it." Marlee pressed a hand to her chest. "I can tell you, though, that Tara feels left out because she's the one without any magical power. I can relate to feeling like an outsider. I'm always the bride's planner, never the bride! Half the people in this town can't even remember my name. I think that helped me pick up on Tara's feelings: we're different but also similar."

I scratched Perkins underneath one wing as I thought back over things Tara had said to me after she realized Hailey was a witch. I had taken it all for frustration, but I trusted Marlee's interpretation, since she was literally feeling the same thing Tara was.

"I'll bring it up with her soon," I promised. It would be awkward, but it might also be healing for both of us. Our relationship had been strained since I'd had a massive magical exhalation at Hailey's dance recital. No one had been hurt by it, but it had been so strong that some people got knocked over from the force of it.

I had also created a panic, because people assumed the concussion that ripped through the auditorium was an earthquake.

Marlee stood up abruptly, which brought me out of my reverie. "I'm going to go outside and shed all of Tara's energy." I had seen Marlee get rid of emotions she'd picked up from others before, and it was even more dramatic than when I did my spell to rid myself of excess magic. Marlee would leave behind a puddle of her dark-red magic, which would slowly dissipate.

"Before you go," I said, reaching out a hand to catch one of Marlee's, "you said that half the town doesn't even remember your name. I'd like to remind you that when you moved in here, you had most of the Foxfire

Haven Fire Department helping you, plus the town's limo driver."

Wyatt hadn't remembered Marlee's name when he'd stopped to talk to her, and when I'd been looking for a roommate, three people had remembered talking to someone about their need for a room, but none of them had remembered it was Marlee. Still, even if there were people around town who found Marlee forgettable, I sure didn't, and neither did a lot of others.

Marlee smiled. "Thanks for the reminder, Haze. Tara's feelings are going to affect me until I get this out of my system. Stella, you're going to help me, right?"

Stella, who was still perched on Marlee's shoulder, clicked her beak three times in rapid succession.

Marlee is being pro-active about the way she's feeling, and I should be, too. Sitting at the table, worrying about Hailey, wasn't going to get me anywhere. I got up and went in search of something productive to do around the house.

I opted for dusting, and I was carefully cleaning off an ornate gilt frame in the back hallway when I heard the front door open. I figured it was just Marlee, but there were clearly two sets of footsteps heading in my direction.

The stern-looking man in the painting whose frame I was dusting peered down at me as Marlee and Valerian appeared.

"I just got home from work," Valerian said. She had an excited gleam in her eyes that I'd come to recognize as her "I've got gossip" look. "Fortie knew he was going to die, all right. Gemma meant it when she said he was aware of his impending doom."

"Give me the details," I said.

"The rumor is that Fortie was going to Melba Hawthorn to help keep death at bay. She's the most expensive witch in town."

Valerian paused dramatically, then added, "She's also the most conniving witch in town."

CHAPTER EIGHT

"YOU CAN SAY THAT again." Marlee gave a firm nod. "Melba Hawthorn has quite the reputation in Foxfire Haven. She's a powerful witch, but don't get in her way."

"Does she do dark magic?" I asked, horrified. That kind of witchcraft wasn't just frowned upon. There were laws in place to make sure witches weren't tempted to do revenge magic or any other kind of unethical working in their craft.

"Nothing like that," Valerian said. "At least, not that I know of. No, it's Melba's business practices you have to watch out for. You know how people talk about getting trapped in a gym membership? She's like that, but with magical consultation contracts. You go to her needing one spell, and you walk out with a monthly membership that you don't need."

"A monthly membership?" I repeated. "For witch-craft?"

"Melba has different tiers," Marlee explained. "One monthly price gets you one spell or potion per month. The next price level gets you three a month, and so on. I kind of admire her for coming up with it, but at the same time, I know too many people who signed one of those contracts without reading the fine print first. They're hard to cancel."

"Besides," Valerian said, "most people don't need that much spell work. We do a lot as a coven, but that's partly to help you relearn your craft, Hazel, and partly because we can. Did we *need* to do that Beautiful House spell of Jo's two weeks ago? No. But did it make this old funeral home look a little brighter and better? Yes."

"If Melba has that kind of reputation, why would Fortie or anyone else go to her?" I asked.

"Because she's good," Marlee said.

"Really good." Valerian lifted a hand, her fingers spread. "I've got five potions behind the bar that some of the tavern patrons swear by. Melba made each one of them. I'm good at making potions, but I have to admit, she's better."

"Fortie was seeing two different witches, Gemma and Melba," I said, "and yet, he died anyway."

"Gemma might be able to predict the future, but she can't change it," Marlee pointed out. "Fortie would have needed Melba for that."

Valerian stared at the painting, but her eyes had an unfocused look. "Imagine knowing you were going to die. Poor Fortie. He ordered my Good Mojo Martini a while back, but he told me it was so he'd get a good cholesterol reading at the doctor the next day."

"Could either one of those witches be Fortie's killer?" I mused.

"Maybe they conspired together," Valerian suggested.

Stella launched herself from Marlee's shoulder and landed on top of the gilt frame, gazing down at the three of us. Marlee looked up at her, then at Valerian and me.

"Someone could have hired one of those witches to kill Fortie with magic, except the constables say it wasn't magic that killed him."

"Gemma and Melba might not be suspects, but I refuse to take Euphoria Lachlan off the list," I said. I explained the conversation I'd overheard between her and the mystery man.

"I hope you told Chief Constable Hightower about that," Valerian said when I'd finished.

"I did. He says neither of them is the killer, based on what I heard. Still, I don't trust Euphoria."

"I never did like her," Marlee muttered.

Before I could ask why, the three of us turned at the sound of the front door opening yet again. A moment later, Jo joined us in the back hallway. "Nothing. I have nothing," she said in greeting, spreading her hands. "There's not a scrap of fresh news about Fortie."

Marlee grumbled softly, then huffed out a breath. "I'm going to have to do another Empathy Erasure spell. Jo, your frustration is hitting me like a tidal wave."

"Sorry, Marlee. I'm frustrated because I stayed at work in the hopes of more news. What a lousy way to spend a Sunday afternoon." Jo inhaled slowly. "I'll go outside with you and do a little relaxation spell. After I get a good night's sleep, I can dive into my assignment first thing tomorrow. My editor wants me to collect quotes from people who knew Fortie."

Valerian laughed. "We've been standing here trying to puzzle out the suspect list, but you might be able to provide one for us! You'll have to tell us if anyone you speak to seems oddly happy."

"Or like they're hiding something," I added.

Jo gave us a little salute. "I'm on the case. But first, it's time to chill."

"While you're working on that story assignment tomorrow," I said, "I plan to make appointments to see both Gemma and Melba. I'll go under the guise of wanting to ensure my delivery business is successful."

"Just don't sign a contract with Melba!" Jo warned me.

I had several deliveries to make on Monday morning, which meant consulting with Gemma and Melba would have to wait. Once I had armed myself with a knit scarf and a water-resistant coat to keep the chilly drizzle at bay, I drove the hearse to Growing Power Garden Store.

The store had become a regular client of mine, but it still felt strange going to the place where I had confronted a killer. Petunia Cornwell wasn't tending to any plants now that she was in jail for Steve Zillmann's murder, but one of her employees had taken over the place.

I found Gnorris behind a desk that was practically hidden by a display of amaryllis plants in colorful pots. Gnorris himself was hardly visible, with just the top half of his face and his tall conical red hat showing above the desktop.

"Good morning, Gnorris," I said to the gnome.

"Hazel, hi." Gnorris's entire face came into view as he clambered up into a standing position on the office chair. His long white beard trailed down over his T-shirt, which was emblazoned with the store's logo. "I've got twenty saplings heading to a cabin out on the coast. It should be a pretty drive for you today."

"I won't be able to see much of anything in this weather," I commented.

Gnorris and another garden store employee helped me load up the hearse, and as I swung the rear door shut, Gnorris leaned toward me. His chin, which was about level with my knee, tilted upward. "What do you think about this murder?"

"I didn't know Fortie, but I hear a lot of people around town disliked him. I wonder if he was killed over something to do with the city council."

"That's my speculation. He liked being the contrarian on the council, so he was always making someone mad. He must have been terrified for his life if he was willing to shell out money to Melba."

"She's supposed to be a very powerful witch."

"She is. She's also a downright shady character." Gnorris chuckled. "Takes one to know one."

"Are you still trying to brew a love potion for the non-magical world?" I gave Gnorris my best stern look, and he squirmed self-consciously.

"No. I don't need a side business anymore. I've got a whole store to myself! Petunia murdering someone was the best thing that ever happened to me." Gnorris tugged on his beard and cleared his throat. "Oh, that doesn't sound nice. What I meant... I'm just saying..."

"Getting to run the garden store is a great opportunity for you," I supplied. "But, yes, you should work on how you phrase it."

Soon, I was underway, the old hearse rolling out of town in the direction of the ocean. I had been right about there not being a lot to see on the drive. The windshield wipers squeaked in protest with every stroke, and orange-and-red leaves skittered across the road in front of me, driven by a growing wind.

I had another delivery after the one for the garden store, and by the time I was finished, I was hungry, cold, and slightly damp.

There was one thing that could take care of two of those problems for me: a grilled-cheese sandwich and tomato soup from The Salt Circle Cafe.

The Salt Circle was named after the practice of pouring a ring of salt— which was impenetrable to ghosts—around oneself for protection. I would never need something like that with a friendly ghost like Holman, but a salt circle could be used as a barrier against malicious spirits. In the case of the cafe, though, it was just a play on words. Their tagline was "Protecting your taste buds since 1947."

The cafe was busy, but I was able to slide into a booth that had just been vacated. Before long, I was happily slurping down a steaming bowl of tomato soup.

As I was dunking a corner of my grilled-cheese sandwich in the soup, a portly man sat down in the booth across the aisle from me. He looked haggard, his face unshaven and his brown hair slightly askew.

A server bustled up to the man and put a hand on his arm. "Newton, what are you doing here at a time like this?"

"I haven't been able to eat. I thought coming here might help. It would at least get me out of the house."

"You poor thing. You want your usual?"

"Yeah. Thanks, Sophie. Plus, I need to order some food for Fortie's wake. My wife made a list." Newton fished a piece of paper out of his jacket pocket and passed it to Sophie.

"All right. Let me get your order in, and then I'll help you out with this list." Sophie moved off, and I saw the way Newton seemed to deflate. He was facing the front windows of the cafe, and his face went from sad to scared as he stared at the street outside.

"I can't stay here!" Newton announced, just as Sophie returned with a cup of coffee for him. He jumped up, looking around wildly. "I was holding it together, but I can't ignore that hearse parked outside. It's an omen. Gemma was right: I'm going to die, too!"

CHAPTER NINE

"NEWTON, WHAT ARE YOU talking about?" Sophie looked from Newton to the front windows, then back to Newton before jerking her chin in my direction. "That's just Dead Easy Delivery, not an omen."

"It is an omen!" Newton insisted. "I went to Gemma last week, before Fortie died, and she saw death for me, too! She was right about Fortie, and she's going to be right about me!"

Newton was breathing rapidly, gasping as his panic rose. The sound of his shallow breaths grew louder, and he began to make a strange sound with each exhale. I couldn't tell if the "err, err" coming out of his mouth was an attempt to speak or not.

I was trying not to stare at the scene Newton was making, but it was impossible to pull my eyes away. I sat and watched, both terrified and fascinated, as his skin began to turn green. His eyes seemed to grow larger, bulging in their sockets.

Sophie put down the cup of coffee and grabbed one of Newton's hands. She reached her other hand out to me. "You're a witch, right? I need help. Just add your calming energy, and I'll do the rest."

I took Sophie's hand and willed myself to feel calm, despite the fact that Newton's throat was beginning to bulge, too. It made me think of the way Gordon's big pelican beak would extend downward when he was eating.

Sophie began to recite something, and I realized she was doing a calming spell. A man sitting at the countertop along the back of the cafe came up with a small round piece of moonstone in one hand. He held it over Newton's head as Sophie continued her spell.

I focused on sending calming energy to both Sophie and Newton. As I did so, I watched Newton's throat begin to contract back down to its normal size. His skin slowly lost its green tint, and his eyes seemed to shrink back into his face.

Sophie dropped my hand and pulled Newton into a hug.

"Sorry," he mumbled. "I wasn't ready to be out and about so soon after Fortie's death. I'll call you later about the food for the wake."

Sophie said something too quiet for me to hear, and then Newton left. She turned to me and nodded appreciatively. "Thanks. Your help kept that from being much worse."

"What was happening to him?" I could hear the way my voice shook. I had been concentrating on sending calming energy, but I had felt fear, too.

"Newton is a shifter," Sophie explained. "And, when his emotions start to spiral out of control, he begins to shift."

"He was turning green," I pointed out. Newton was definitely not a werewolf.

Sophie looked grim. "Poor guy is a bullfrog shifter."

A werefrog? I wanted to ask how, exactly, that worked. If Sophie hadn't intervened, would Newton have shrunk down until he looked like a typical bullfrog, or would he have been a human-sized one? I screwed up my face as I imagined a giant frog perched in the aisle next to where I was sitting.

"That's how most of us feel about it," Sophie said, noticing my expression. "What a shame he couldn't have been something cool. I used to date a werepossum, and I thought that was embarrassing. At least he wasn't a frog."

"Newton and Fortie were close, I take it," I said.

"Like brothers. They used to have lunch here twice a week."

"I am sorry that my hearse made Newton start to shift." I had gotten some strange reactions to the hearse, but "bad omen" was a first.

"Not your fault," Sophie assured me. "Newton is grieving, and if that pea reader has been foretelling death for him, then he was primed to panic."

That reminded me I had planned to make appointments with both Gemma and Melba. Once Sophie moved off, I pulled out my phone and searched for Gemma's information online. I couldn't find anything, and as I paid for my lunch, I mentioned it to Sophie.

"She's not that high-tech," Sophie said. "Just show up at her house, and she's either on the clock or not." Sophie rattled off an address for a place on the north end of town.

No one was at the funeral home when I returned, so I texted my roommates and asked if they wanted to join me in a visit to Gemma. I got a swift *yes* from Jo and Marlee, and Valerian texted about fifteen minutes later to say she'd go with us if we planned it during her dinner break at the tavern.

We agreed to Valerian's timeframe, and Jo texted, *I'll bring the peas!*

With that settled, I went to the room that had been Uncle Grant's office. It felt strange sitting behind the hulking desk, especially when my laptop was so small, but the thing was so gigantic I didn't want to deal with moving it.

Unlike Gemma, Melba did have a website. It was a slick design full of the kind of marketing speak I would expect from a big corporation, not a small-town witch.

Unfortunately for me, though, Melba's online booking system showed that she had no available appointments for the next three weeks. She might have a reputation for being a bit of a shady business woman, but she was definitely popular.

I spent my afternoon doing small tasks around the house. When I had first moved in, I had loathed the idea of needing roommates in order to afford all the necessary repairs to the place. Now that I was used to having the three other women around, the old funeral home felt too big when it was just me at home.

Well, Perkins, Holman, and me. But since Perkins was an eight-inch-tall burrowing owl and Holman was a ghost, I wasn't sure how much either of them counted. Perkins took good care of me, but I couldn't have a conversation with him about my adventure at The Salt Circle.

The house felt a lot more full once Jo and Marlee were home. Gordon usually stayed home while Jo was at the newspaper office, but he'd followed her there that morning. Now that Jo and Gordon were back, he padded down the hallway on his big webbed feet as Jo headed for her room at the back of the house.

If Newton had continued shifting, he would have had webbed feet, too.

I made a gagging noise and tried not to think about it.

Soon, Marlee was driving us to the address I had for Gemma. Valerian was going to meet us there.

Gemma's house was a tall, narrow place that looked like it had been built in the Victorian era. There was even a small turret tacked onto one corner. The blue paint was peeling, and the lawn was covered with pinwheels that spun wildly in the breeze.

I was so busy taking in all the details of the house and yard that I didn't notice the most important thing until Marlee pointed it out. There was a line of people stretching from the front door, down the porch steps, and halfway to the street.

Valerian had arrived just ahead of us, and she looked pointedly at her watch. "I already know my future, and it's working this double shift. I'm willing to wait, but I might have to head back to work before we get inside."

"I'm not excited about standing in line, but I already got the peas." Jo held up the plastic bag of frozen peas as proof. She had stopped at the store on her way home from the newspaper office.

"Is Gemma always this busy?" I asked as the four of us joined the end of the line.

A woman standing in front of me turned around. "It's been like this since Fortie died. Everyone wants to know if they'll be next!" The woman's ominous expression was so dramatic I almost laughed at her, but I managed to give her a solemn nod, instead.

"Murder is a strange business plan," Valerian said under her breath, "but could Gemma have killed Fortie herself to boost business?"

"I thought she was just a harmless old bat," Jo said.

"Petunia made bridal bouquets for my clients for years, and she turned out to be a killer," Marlee pointed out. "You just never know about people."

The front door cracked open just then, and a man strode out with a grin on his face. He paused on the porch and thumped a hand against his chest. "I won't be dying anytime soon!"

A few people in line clapped politely, and others offered their congratulations.

Two women went inside the house next. They were clutching each other's hands as they mounted the porch steps, like they were afraid of what might happen inside. The line shuffled forward a couple of feet.

"I sure hope thawed peas can tell the future as well as frozen ones," Jo said in a bored tone.

Valerian sighed and looked at her watch again.

I was staring at the front door, wondering just how long I was willing to stand in line for something that was seeming more silly by the minute, when I heard a man say my name. I turned around to see Wyatt and another constable standing there.

The other man, Callan, had also been with Wyatt when the constables had come to take care of the body in my garage. Callan smiled at me, but Wyatt gave me his trademark glare. "Are you still sticking your nose into constable business?" he asked me.

"We're here to consult with Gemma," I said.
"Well, we're here to investigate a murder."

CHAPTER TEN

"So you're here in an official capacity?" I asked in a mock-innocent tone. I had told the truth about us being at Gemma's to have our peas read, but Wyatt had also been correct in assuming I had an ulterior motive. I wouldn't have been standing there in front of the house if it weren't for my curiosity about Fortie and his murder.

"Of course." Wyatt tilted his head slightly. "Why else would I be here?"

"You could be looking for insight into your future," I pointed out. Even as I said it, I knew how ridiculous it was. Wyatt Hightower was not the kind of man to turn to a bag of frozen peas for guidance.

Wyatt narrowed his eyes at me. Somehow, they seemed even more brilliantly blue as he stared me down, and I felt a little shiver run up my back. I hated to be the one to give up in our staring contest, but I couldn't take it for more than a few seconds, so I turned my head away with a frustrated huff.

"We really did come to get our peas read," Valerian said. She seemed to think Wyatt hadn't been convinced I wasn't there to stick my nose into the murder investigation. "We had no idea Gemma was a suspect."

"What makes you think she's a suspect?" Wyatt snapped. This time, it was Valerian who was on the receiving end of his stare.

Unlike me, though, Valerian wasn't going to back down. She shrugged casually. "You said you were here on official business, and we know Fortie's death was foretold by Gemma. Maybe she saw death in his future because she was the one plotting his murder."

Callan's face began to twitch. At first, I thought he was trying to hold in a sneeze, but then I realized he was making an effort not to laugh at Valerian's smart guess. He pressed the fingers of one hand against his lips as his eyes slid toward Wyatt.

Who, of course, didn't find it funny.

"And Val is right," Marlee chimed in. "We were talking about Gemma's skills before we even knew about the murder."

"We even brought our own peas!" Jo held up the bag and gave it a little shake.

"Then I'm afraid you'll have to wait a bit before you can learn your futures, ladies," Wyatt said. "This might take a while. In fact, it's best if you just head on home."

Jo shook the bag again. "But I already bought the peas!"

"I'm sorry." Wyatt, to my surprise, looked like he meant it.

Wyatt and Callan moved on, slowly working their way toward the front door as they told the other people in line they shouldn't bother waiting. Once we reached the sidewalk, Valerian checked her watch yet again. "I don't have a lot of time left, but I can get a quick dinner with you three."

"I can't believe you're working a double again," Marlee said. "Is Hazel charging you too much rent?"

Valerian winked at me. "She's not charging me nearly enough for that sweet chapel room. But I'm not doing it for the money. Our nighttime guy claims he's too grief-stricken about Fortie to come into work tonight."

Based on the look of distaste on Valerian's face, she didn't believe that for one minute.

Jo suggested we go to Back to Realitea, which was just off Main Street and only a short walk from the tavern. Before long, we were seated around a small round table inside one of the cutest little spaces I'd seen since moving back to Foxfire Haven, though I had to admit it bordered on ridiculous. There was lace everywhere: hanging in the windows as curtains, draped over the mint-green tablecloths, displayed in frames on the walls, and even worked into the collar of the black-and-white cat who was perched on one of the built-in window seats.

The chairs were all wide and squishy, and I sat back in mine as I observed the tearoom. Only two other tables were occupied, so I had a nice view of the floral wallpaper—which matched the tablecloths—and the antique photos of women drinking tea while dressed much fancier than we were.

"I don't remember this place from when I was a kid," I commented as I eyed a display of scones.

"It opened about fifteen years ago," Marlee said. "A lot of my wedding clients have their bridal showers here."

"Would Gemma have seen petit fours in our future?" Jo mused. "We'll never know."

"Wyatt must consider her a suspect," Valerian said. "I wasn't just making a wild speculation. The constables already know she foresaw his death in the peas, so the only reason they would be there again is if they think Gemma might have done it."

"If she doesn't wind up in jail, I'd still like to pay her a visit," I said. "How about tomorrow evening?"

Marlee pulled her phone from her purse and gazed at the screen. "I've got a meeting with a client tomorrow. Maybe the day after?"

"Yeah, let's do Wednesday," Valerian said. "I'm off that day."

We paused our planning to order our teas, then got back to settling on a time Wednesday for our coven outing to Gemma's house. Once our small pots of tea and a tower of petit fours, scones, and finger sandwiches arrived, we moved on to talking about things that had nothing to do with peas or Fortie's murder.

As I spread clotted cream over my scone, I felt a wave of gratitude. I was enjoying a nice evening with my friends, and I didn't have to hide my magic or be anyone other than my true self with them. Plus, the food was delicious, so that added to my joy.

Valerian headed back to the tavern after scarfing down her share of the food, but the rest of us lingered for a while. It was nearly dark out, and raindrops were lazily falling outside while a few leaves skittered past on the sidewalk. We were much happier staying inside Back to Realitea with our hot tea and comfortable chairs.

Eventually, though, it was time to head home. The cold drizzle did little to dampen our spirits as we spilled out the door.

Once we got home, I called for Perkins, but he was nowhere to be found. In fact, I realized, all of the familiars were missing. I alerted Jo and Marlee, and soon, the three of us were roaming the old funeral home, calling the names of our birds.

An angry caw echoed from somewhere above, and Marlee carefully went up the steep, narrow staircase that led to the attic. "Up here," she called to Jo and me. "Bring some towels."

I grabbed a couple of towels from the bathroom and returned in time to see Jo disappearing into the attic. I didn't like climbing the rickety old stairs, and I'd only been up into the attic once since moving in. I threw the towels over my shoulder, steeled myself, and began to take the steps slowly.

When Marlee let out a sound that was something between a squeak and a scream, I moved a lot faster, worried something was wrong. When I emerged into the spacious attic, though, I saw she was laughing.

She was also wet.

"They're all soaked," Marlee explained as I stepped up next to her and Jo. "Gordon must have decided I should be, too, because he stretched out his wings and shook off about a gallon of water onto my head."

I gazed upward, toward the peaked ceiling. Our four familiars were huddled together on a rafter, looking dejected. I pulled one of the towels off my shoulder and spread it out in my hands. "Who's first?"

Perkins fluttered down, landing right in the middle of the towel. I folded it around him and rubbed gently as he closed his eyes and lifted his head. When he made a soft cooing noise, I loosened the towel, and he made the short flight to my shoulder.

Jo grabbed the other towel and offered it to Marlee. "Sorry Gordon got you."

Marlee ran the towel down her face and dabbed at her sweater. "It's pretty funny, actually. The poor things must have been flying outside, and they got stuck in this rain. The broken attic window was probably the nearest escape from it."

Lonnie, Valerian's raven, flew down toward me so I could dry her while Marlee dried her toucan. "Poor Stella," Marlee kept repeating.

Gordon was last. He was too big for us to hold while we dried him, so he perched on the floor while both Jo and Marlee rubbed him down with the towels. He squawked loudly the entire time.

"Oh, don't be such a baby," Jo admonished. "You're a pelican. You dive into water, you float on water, and you love being near the water. Now you want to complain about being wet?"

Gordon didn't answer the question, but he did stop complaining after that.

I had been fine dashing through the rain when we left the tea shop, but the attic was cold and damp, and I felt a chill creeping into my bones as I slowly descended the stairs. Once I got Perkins settled into his nest of flannel scraps next to the kitchen radiator, I took a hot shower to warm myself up.

Before I went to bed that night, I checked on Perkins. He looked warm and content, and Stella was nestled next to him. I bent down and gave Perkins a kiss on the head, then stroked Stella's black wings. "Good night, you two."

I had just turned off the lamp on my nightstand, when my phone rang. I always worried when someone called me that late, but I relaxed after I saw Valerian's name on the screen. I assumed she was simply calling to pass along some gossip.

"Hey, Val," I answered. "Everything good?"

"Busy." I could hear the hum of voices in the background, and I had to concentrate to understand Valerian when she spoke again, because she was clearly trying to talk without being overheard. "That man you heard talking to Euphoria. Did he sound like this?"

A few seconds later, one of the voices began to stand out from the rest, and I knew Valerian was holding her phone in the person's direction. It was a deep voice, and I quickly recognized it as belonging to the man who wanted to write a thank-you note to Fortie's killer. He was saying something about his favorite baseball team.

The man's voice faded, and soon, Val said, "So?"

"That's the same guy. How did you guess?"

"Because he's in here having a drink with Mayor Lachlan. The man who's so happy about Fortie's murder is Julian Ashcroft. And he's on the city council, too!"

CHAPTER ELEVEN

I GASPED AT VALERIAN'S news before I laughed. "Val, what would I do without you? You always have the good gossip!"

"You've got a newspaper reporter and a bartender in your life, so you'll never be in the dark about what's happening in Foxfire Haven." I could hear the pride in Valerian's voice. She liked having a job that allowed her to know so much of what was happening in our town. "Anyway, Julian is a creep. He's as greasy as the burgers they serve at his grill down the street."

I wrinkled my nose. It was probably the place where Wyatt had gotten his smelly burger. "Remind me not to eat there."

"I don't know what happened between him and Fortie, but I'm guessing it was some kind of city council clash."

I nodded, even though Valerian couldn't see me. "That's likely. And of course Julian is a creep. No one nice would be buddies with Euphoria."

"She's a terrible tipper. Okay, I have to go. Barry's whiskey glass is empty. But I'll stick close to the mayor and Julian to see if they say anything about Fortie." Valerian hung up, and I could picture her scooting to the end of the bar to refill the Bigfoot's drink.

The next morning, I shuffled into the kitchen and found Jo at the table, her coffee mug nearly empty already. She smiled and said brightly, "Good morning, Hazel! I hope you slept well."

I nodded and mumbled an affirmative. Jo's biggest flaw was being a morning person. Once I had filled my own coffee mug, I topped hers off and sat down at the table. After a few minutes and a few sips, I was finally awake enough to talk coherently. "What do you know about Julian Ashcroft?"

Jo looked confused for a moment, then her eyes lit up. "He's a suspect in Fortie's murder, isn't he?"

"He's the man I overheard talking to Euphoria about how Fortie's death was a good thing. Wyatt says Julian can't be the killer, because he was talking to Euphoria like someone else had done it, but I'm not writing him off."

Jo tapped a long finger against her mug as she thought. "Julian is a real piece of work. I'll pull some articles about his antics on the city council. How did you figure out he was the one talking to the mayor, anyway?"

"Val saw the two of them at the tavern last night, and she put it together."

"And another question."

I laughed and raised a hand. "I haven't had enough coffee yet to give an interview."

Jo leaned forward and propped her chin in her hand as she gazed at me. "Why do you care about this murder so much? It seems like your interest goes beyond casual curiosity, but you didn't even know Fortie."

"I'm not sure, to tell you the truth," I said slowly. "Though, if I had to give you an answer, I'd say it's because I might not have known Fortie, but I do know Euphoria. I really want to find out if she was complicit in his murder."

"She was a real jerk to you back when you were kids, wasn't she?"

"Yeah."

"Maybe I'll pull a few past articles that shed her in a bad light, too." Jo grinned at me wickedly. "It will make you feel better."

"I'm not that bitter," I said, my smile matching Jo's. "At least, I don't think I am."

Jo left a few minutes later to finish getting ready for her day at the newspaper office. I was enjoying the last of my coffee while reciting a spell Marlee had come up with called Start the Day Right, when my phone rang.

"I'd like to hire your delivery service to take some things to the thrift store in Stanton," the man on the other end said. The voice was familiar to me, but I couldn't quite place it.

"Sure. Thanks for calling Dead Easy Delivery! Who am I speaking with?"

There was a pause, then the man said, "It's not important. I won't be at home when you come to pick the things up, and I'm a very private person."

I wasn't quite sure how to respond to that. If the client wouldn't even tell me who they were, then how would I be able to bill them for the work?

My mystery customer must have been thinking the same thing, because he said, "The items will be on my front porch, and if you tell me how much I owe you, I'll leave cash in an envelope, too."

I gave him the quote for running a hearse-load of stuff all the way to Stanton. There was a secondhand store in Foxfire Haven, and I wondered if the man had chosen a place the next town over, instead, to protect his privacy even further. Not only was it a bigger town, but it wasn't magical, and people in Foxfire Haven tended to go to Stanton only when they absolutely had to.

Because, as magical people, we had to be secretive about our abilities. My misgivings about having a client who wouldn't identify himself began to lift. He was a private person, like so many others in Foxfire Haven. I couldn't blame him for not wanting to do anything that might subject him to local gossip.

I got up and rummaged in the junk drawer to find a scrap of paper, then wrote down the client's address. We settled on a day and time for me to pick up the items for delivery, and I promised to be discreet before thanking the man for the business.

"Why would someone need privacy just because they're downsizing a bit?" I asked Perkins after ending the call.

Perkins cooed in answer, which I took to mean he didn't know.

There were people in Foxfire Haven who loved to gossip about my uncle and his strange behavior in the years before his death. Perhaps Uncle Grant had gotten a bit strange, but he wasn't the only one in this town.

Still, though, business was business, and I was grateful for every job I got for Dead Easy Delivery.

The last of my coffee had cooled during the phone call, so I reluctantly turned my mind to the things I needed to do around the house that morning. Laundry was at the top of the list, followed by an attempt to get decades-old grease splatters off the tile behind the stove.

I wasn't looking forward to either of those tasks. To make the housework more palatable, I turned on an old radio I'd found in Grant's office and tuned it to a local rock station. Before long, I was bouncing my head in time to the music while scrubbing the tile.

After lunch, I had started rolling up my sleeves to continue working on tasks around the house, when Marlee called and asked if I could do a last-minute delivery that afternoon. I quickly agreed, eager for the excuse not to do housework, and I was surprised when she said it would be for Fortie's memorial celebration that night.

"It's all very last-minute," Marlee told me. "The funeral is going to be on Friday, but that's only for family and close friends. Mayor Lachlan felt there should be a place for the public to honor Fortie."

Of course she did. Euphoria was determined to look like the kind, compassionate mayor. Still, I congratulated Marlee on getting the gig.

"The deputy mayor is an acquaintance of mine," Marlee said. "He called and asked if I'd be willing to help with a few details, despite it being a same-day thing. And, since the city is in a pinch to get it done, he also said they'd pay me double my usual rate."

"You and I are going to be two rich witches with all this work!"

The cargo I was going to be delivering to the park, where the memorial would be held, was the most unusual thing I'd been asked to transport yet. Marlee asked me to drive to a small warehouse a short way outside of town to pick up magical, non-flammable fireworks. I had no idea how they worked, but I was looking forward to seeing them in action.

If I even attended the memorial. As Jo had pointed out just that morning, I hadn't even known Fortie.

The warehouse where the fireworks were stored was also where they were made. The rusted metal warehouse was at the end of a dirt lane, and a faded sign above the tall roll-up door proclaimed it was the Foxfire Haven Firework Factory.

As I pulled to a stop near the door, I saw a brilliant flash of blue directly in front of me. It was followed by an explosion of glittering yellow sparks that fanned out to look like a flower. I gasped with delight. Not only were these magical fireworks nonflammable, but they didn't *boom* like traditional fireworks, either. Instead, they made a high-pitched humming noise that reminded me of the way Marlee sounded when she sipped her favorite tea after a long day of putting on an event for a client.

"Pretty even in the daytime, aren't they?"

I turned to see a lanky man walking toward me from the far side of the warehouse. His denim overalls were faded and streaked with black, and when he lifted his camouflage cap in greeting, I spotted the long, tapered tips of his ears peeking out from his curly gray hair.

It wasn't just the fireworks that were magical. Their maker was an elf.

A country elf, at that. The man came to a stop, hooked his thumbs in the straps of his overalls, and tilted his head toward the warehouse. "I'm Sable, and you must be Hazel. I've got everything ready to go. I have to say I'm surprised, though. Fortie Fortenbacher wasn't exactly the most popular guy."

"That's what I keep hearing. I just moved back to Foxfire Haven, so I never met him."

"He lived on the outside for a couple years, you know." Sable said it in a half whisper, his arched eyebrows waggling over his turquoise eyes. "Phoenix."

"Fortie was a phoenix?" I asked, surprised. They were one of the rarest of magical beings, if I was remembering my grade-school education correctly.

"No, I mean Fortie lived in Phoenix, Arizona." Sable shook his head. "Why anyone would want to live in the outside world is beyond me. Too many people and not enough nature."

I bristled at the comment, since I had lived in the "outside world" for thirty years. I had loved San Francisco, and I had been sad to leave when I realized I needed to take my wayward magic back to a town that wouldn't panic if I had a little exhalation.

Or a big one, as was more likely for me.

Instead of trying to explain the perks of big-city life to an elf, though, I gestured at the trees surrounding the warehouse. "You certainly have an abundance of nature here."

"That I do, and I'd like to keep it that way." Sable led me toward the roll-up door as he continued, "I like being away from the world. Can you imagine what would happen if a non-magical person spotted my fireworks?"

Just like my mystery client, Sable liked his privacy. It seemed to be a theme for my day.

Sable continued chatting as he helped me load boxes of fireworks into the back of the hearse. He gave me a brief explanation about how they worked, but he used terms I hadn't heard in decades, and, eventually, I gave up trying to understand. I chalked the fireworks up to advanced elven magic. They weren't something my coven would be making anytime in the near future.

Before leaving the warehouse, I texted Marlee to let her know I'd be at the park in about twenty minutes. She was going to meet me so we could unload the fireworks. When I arrived at the park, I was astonished to see a huge crowd standing in the grass around the gazebo. Even finding a place to park the hearse was difficult, and I had to squeeze into a spot a block away.

"I need to buy a handcart," I grumbled as I climbed out of the hearse.

"We can use mine," Marlee said as she stepped up next to me. I spotted her car across the street. "I'll go grab it."

As we loaded some of the boxes onto the handcart, I nodded in the direction of the park. "Are we late?"

"No. The memorial ceremony isn't until tonight." Marlee plopped a box onto the top of the stack. "Let's take this load over, then come back for the rest."

When we walked into the park, I saw why people were standing around the gazebo. There was a podium set up at the top of the steps, and Euphoria was standing behind it, speaking into a microphone.

"...so happy to announce we already have a candidate to replace Fortie Fortenbacher on the city council," she was saying as Marlee and I got within hearing range.

"Of course, we'll have to wait for the special election to know for sure it's his seat, but I think we all know what a great councilman Newton Yates will be!"

CHAPTER TWELVE

THE GATHERED CROWD BEGAN to applaud politely as Euphoria smiled down at all of them. Her chestnut waves shimmered in the late-afternoon light that slanted into the gazebo, and her gray tweed coat and red scarf made her the most posh-looking person in the park.

Beside me, Marlee made a *tsk* sound. "Someone is already gunning for Fortie's seat on the city council? That's not a good look, when Fortie's body isn't even in the ground yet."

"Not just someone," I said. "Newton was Fortie's best friend! Just yesterday, at The Salt Circle, he was so upset about the murder that he started to shift into his bullfrog form right there in front of everyone."

"Frog? Yuck. Do you think he eats flies when he's in that form?" Marlee shook her head violently, her ponytail whipping from side to side. "Nope. I can't even think about that. How interesting, though, that Euphoria is so quick to back Newton as Fortie's replacement."

I suddenly giggled, and a few people near us turned to glare. They either thought I was being disrespectful to Euphoria or to Fortie's memory.

It was the former. I nudged Marlee and said under my breath, "The princess and the frog."

As far as I was concerned, Euphoria was still a suspect in the murder, even though Wyatt had said both she and Julian must be innocent. She had apparently disliked Fortie, and now, she was wasting no time to support a candidate to replace him. Had she gotten Fortie out of the way so she could get someone she liked onto the city council? Maybe she and Newton had made a deal that he'd help her out with city business if she backed his candidacy.

I heard a loud exhale and rapid footsteps across the grass, and I looked over to see Jo dashing up to us. "What did I miss?" she asked breathlessly.

"Mayor Lachlan doing some political maneuvering," Marlee said.

"She's backing Newton Yates to replace Fortie on the city council," I added.

Jo's face clouded over. "We need to talk. Now."

"We can't." Marlee patted the pile of fireworks boxes on her handcart. "We have to deliver all these fireworks, plus more that are still in the hearse."

"Let's go to the tavern," Jo suggested. "By the time we're done, all these people will have cleared out, and it will be easier to unload."

Marlee and I agreed, and after we stashed the hand-cart and its contents in the corner of the park where volunteers were already setting up for the memorial, we followed Jo across the street to Sit a Spell Tavern.

The tavern was mostly empty, which wasn't a surprise, since it was the middle of the afternoon. Besides, anyone on their way to the tavern had probably stopped to see what the hubbub in the park was all about. We easily found stools at the bar.

Valerian came up to us with a knowing look. "You're not here for beer."

Jo was already pulling out a manila file folder, putting it on the bar like we were at a business meeting rather than a tavern. "No. I came to share some things I found while digging through back issues of the newspaper."

"Val, where's your biggest customer today?" I asked. Usually, I spotted Barry during the daytime.

"He came and went already. Maybe he's getting over whatever he's been sulking about."

"Good for him but bad for your whiskey sales."

Jo laid three sheets of paper out in a row, and I saw they were all photocopies of newspaper articles. "Hazel, I did what you asked and looked for older stories that mentioned Julian and his work on the city council. In the process, though, I found something even more interesting. Euphoria had good reason to dislike Fortie. Look."

The first article had the ominous title of *Clash Over Camp*. Jo had highlighted a few key points, and she tapped a finger against the paper. "This one is about an old camp, out near the coast."

"Camp Arcane!" I exclaimed. "I used to go there every summer as a kid."

"I hate to break it to you, but it's been closed for years," Valerian said.

"Right. But Mayor Lachlan wanted to fix it up and reopen it," Jo continued. "Most of the council agreed with the plan, but Fortie was against it. He argued the children of Foxfire Haven could go to any of the dozen or so other camps in this area."

"Except those camps are run by non-magical peo-ple," Marlee pointed out. "Kids from here would have to hide their magic."

"And if one of them slipped..." I shuddered at the idea. After my big incident at Hailey's dance recital, I could just imagine the chaos that would result from a kid accidentally unleashing magic in a camp cafeteria full of ten-year-olds.

"Exactly. Fortie and Euphoria went head-to-head over it." Jo pointed at the next piece of paper she'd laid on the bar. "And this article details their fight over an issue with how business licenses are doled out."

The next story Jo had found was about a debate Euphoria and Fortie had gotten into during a city council meeting, when the town's historic inn had been asking for approval to build an addition that broke a few of Foxfire Haven's historic district guide-lines.

Jo slapped a palm against the file folder. "There's more, but this gives you an idea how much they dis-liked each other. Euphoria having a candidate to back just days after Fortie's murder is very suspicious."

I was shaking my head before Jo had even finished. "If Euphoria and Fortie were that contentious, then why would she be so enthusiastic about supporting his best friend as a candidate? It doesn't make sense."

"Hazel has a point," Valerian said. "If Euphoria killed Fortie—or had someone do it for her—then it seems like she'd pick a different replacement for his city council spot."

"Just because they were best friends doesn't mean they had identical views," Marlee pointed out.

"Either way, Newton looks as suspicious as Euphoria," I said. "He's jumping in to replace Fortie before there's even been a funeral."

Marlee burst out laughing. "Jumping? Like a frog?"

"I promise, that was an unintentional joke." Even still, I laughed before I turned to Jo. "You know what you have to do with this information, right?"

Jo nodded. "I'm taking it straight over to the constables. Unlike you, I'm not afraid of Chief Constable Hightower."

"I am not afraid of him! I just don't like him."

"But you're a little afraid of him, too." Jo leaned in close and curled her hands around her eyes, like she was holding an invisible pair of binoculars. "You're worried he'll stare you down with those sexy blue eyes."

"They are not sexy," I muttered. As a matter of fact, I thought Wyatt's eyes were gorgeous. He was a handsome man, but there was no way I was going to admit it to anyone.

Jo gathered up the articles she'd found and headed out. Marlee and Valerian told her to have a good afternoon, while I wished her luck.

She'd need it if she was going to get Wyatt to listen to her about Euphoria being a suspect.

Marlee and I headed back to the park, but Jo had been wrong about the crowd dispersing while we were chatting inside the tavern. The crowd was still nearly as big, and people were standing in close groups, talking excitedly. I figured they were all discussing the mayor's announcement and probably coming up with their own theories about Fortie's murder.

It didn't take us long to get the rest of the fireworks unloaded, and after we'd dropped off the last of the boxes at the staging area, Marlee and I lingered a bit. She had run into someone she knew, and as they caught up, I moved closer to the nearest group to see if I could hear what they were discussing.

I was disappointed to find they were only talking about a new burger at Foxfire Grill. Hopefully, it was something less stinky than the one Wyatt had been eating a few days before.

After Marlee finished her chat, she grabbed the handcart, and we began to weave our way through the clustered groups. It was getting late enough in the day that I wondered if many of the people would stay in the park to attend Fortie's memorial, which would start in just an hour.

Again, I debated going, then decided against it. I was tired, and I wasn't really excited to be at yet another event where I'd risk running into Euphoria.

Marlee and I had nearly reached the street when Newton stepped right in front of us, bringing us to an abrupt halt. "Hello, ladies!" he said brightly. His wide smile made me think of a toad, and I had to remind myself he wasn't a toad but a bullfrog, at least sometimes.

What's the difference between a toad and a bull-frog, anyway? I wondered.

I didn't have time to think about the answer, because Newton was still talking. "I hope the two of you will consider voting for me when—oh. It's you." Newton was looking at me with a mixture of surprise and embarrassment.

"Hello, Newton. We didn't meet properly at The Salt Circle. I'm Hazel Underwood."

"She owns Dead Easy Delivery," Marlee added.

"Ah, yes," Newton said tightly. "The hearse is yours."

"I'm sorry if seeing it the other day upset you."

Newton drew in a deep breath, then let it out in a loud rush. "It did, but I'm feeling much better now. I appreciate you helping Sophie with that calming spell."

"I was happy to help. Here's what I don't get, Newton. You said at the cafe that you thought your own death was imminent, so why bother to run for city council?"

Newton smiled again, and it looked more genuine this time. His toad-like grin, I decided, was reserved for trying to win people over. This was a real smile, and it was far less disconcerting. "I want to honor Fortie's legacy by continuing his work on the city council. Besides, I visited Gemma again last night. As it turns out, I'm not going to die, after all. I'm going to live a long, prosperous life!"

CHAPTER THIRTEEN

MARLEE AND I EXCHANGED a quick glance, then looked back at Newton. "But you said Gemma had seen death in your frozen peas," I pointed out.

"She did," Newton confirmed. "So, last night, I went back to her, hoping she'd have some insight into how much time I had left. But she no longer saw death. In fact, the peas foretold success for me. Gemma says I must have altered my fate for the better, because the signs had shifted."

"How did you alter your fate?" Marlee asked.

Newton shrugged affably. "Who knows? Maybe my decision to pick up where Fortie left off is what did it. Perhaps honoring his legacy is what's allowing me to live."

In my mind, I saw the articles Jo had printed out. If Newton was planning to do just as he'd said, that implied Euphoria wouldn't get along with him any better than she had with Fortie. "Where, exactly," I asked, "did Fortie leave off? What kinds of things did he support? What was he pushing for on the city council?"

Newton's grin slipped downward. "Well, um. Fortie believed... He supported..." He paused, glanced away, then cleared his throat. "The point is, I'm going to be a good advocate for our town and its people! Can I count on your vote, ladies?"

Instead of answering, Marlee pointed at Newton. "You were best friends with Fortie. Maybe you can tell me why he had one of my Enchanted Events cards on him, and why it had something about a birthday ritual written on it."

Newton's body language changed instantly. After the discomfort of clearly having no idea what Fortie's work on the city council had involved, he was happy to shift to a topic he knew something about. "He was going to try a ritual designed to lengthen his life. But it was a ritual that had to be performed on his birthday, and he didn't even make it that far. He was born in February."

"But why was it written on one of my business cards?" Marlee pressed.

"You just mentioned your business is Enchanted Events. She told Fortie a ritual like this would require the energy of a lot of people—we're talking about cheating death, after all—and I expect he would have needed help planning it. It would have been a birthday party combined with the ritual, so you can imagine all the details that would have gone into it."

"You said 'she' told Fortie the ritual would take a lot of energy," I said. "Who is she?"

"Melba Hawthorn." Newton said it like it should have been obvious. "Fortie went to her for years, and lately, he was getting her magical help to prevent his death. Melba is the one who suggested the ritual. Of course, none of her spells or charms made a difference in the end, did they? He died anyway, just like the peas predicted."

"Let me guess," I said. "Fortie would have hired Marlee to plan the birthday party, and he would have hired Melba to show up and conduct the ritual to extend his life."

"Exactly." Newton pressed his hand to his chest. "But we'll never know if it would have worked."

A man wearing a crisp white Oxford shirt and khaki pants moved toward us, and his grin was as wide as Newton's as he reached out a hand to shake both Marlee's and mine. "Hello, hello. Thank you for coming out to honor Fortie tonight."

I had never met the man, but I instantly recognized his voice. When I told him my name, he didn't bother to give me his. He probably figured he was well-known enough in Foxfire Haven that he didn't need to tell me he was Julian Ashcroft.

Julian threw an arm around Newton's shoulders. "I'm glad to see you're talking to my boy Newton, here. Isn't he great? Born and raised in Foxfire Haven, and ready to fight for this town's future! You can count on him to do a great job keeping our town safe and successful."

Newton's announcement that Gemma had seen success in his future repeated in my mind, and I gave Julian a small smile. "Things do seem to be looking up for Newton," I said.

"We expect great things from him. Soon, we'll all be wishing he'd gone into politics sooner." Julian slapped Newton hard on the back, and I thought I caught just a hint of a green tinge in Newton's skin. Was he more uncomfortable about the situation than his wide smile implied?

Fearing another episode like the one I'd witnessed at The Salt Circle, I took a step back as I gestured toward the handcart. "It was nice talking to you both, but Marlee and I should really be going."

"We'll see you tonight at the memorial," Newton said. "I worked really hard on my speech about Fortie."

"Looking forward to it," Marlee said, even though she'd mentioned to me that she also had no interest in attending. I doubted either man would notice our absence, anyway.

Newton and Julian moved off, stopping at a nearby group of young men. The smiling and shaking hands began again, and Julian's voice carried to where Marlee and I were standing. *He could have had a lucrative career as a sports announcer,* I thought.

"Newton might be a bullfrog shifter, but Julian is the slimy one," Marlee said quietly. She was looking toward the two men with an expression of mild disgust.

"Had you ever met him before?"

"Yeah, he's been at some of the events I coordinated. He never remembers who I am, even though we've met four or five times now. It's impossible for me to forget him, though, because he gives off such a feeling of false-hood."

"You're the empath," I said. "Did you get a guilty feeling that might indicate whether Julian had anything to do with Fortie's murder?"

"It's hard for me to pick up the emotions of people like him. He's got that slimy, fake-friendly facade locked into place so hard that it's like a barrier in front of his real feelings. For all I know, he was standing there, talking up Newton, all while thinking he'd rather be at home digging into a pint of mint-chip ice cream."

"I'd rather be doing that," I said wistfully.

"Then let's get to it! Our work here is done. The city hired me to coordinate the fireworks, not to stick around and watch them."

I walked Marlee to her car to help load the handcart into the back of it, and after she closed the rear of her compact SUV, she turned and leaned against it, a thoughtful look on her face. "How much money do you think Melba was going to charge Fortie for that birthday ritual?"

"If the rumors about her pricing are true, then I'm going to guess it would have cost Fortie an arm and a leg."

Marlee snickered. "Better to lose those than your entire life, I suppose."

"And just think of the audience Melba would have had for the ritual. A huge birthday party, and all those potential customers watching her save Fortie's life with magic."

"That means Melba is not a suspect, right? Surely she wouldn't have killed Fortie before doing that lucrative of a gig for him."

I hitched up a shoulder. "Maybe he paid in advance."

Both of us snickered that time, and Marlee mumbled something about us being disrespectful to the dead. She didn't sound that remorseful about it, but we did stop making bad jokes about the situation.

"I'll see you at home," Marlee said. She turned away from me and moved toward the driver's side of her car, but she stopped abruptly and faced me again. "I still don't understand how my card wound up in Fortie's pocket. I've never even met Melba. It's nice to know people around town are recommending my business, but I would really like to find out how she happened to have one of my cards in the first place."

"It's a mystery," I agreed.

I waved as Marlee climbed into the driver's seat, then dashed across the street to the hearse. It had been a strange encounter in the park. Newton, who had been so upset about Fortie's death at the Salt Circle, was suddenly acting like the hopeful politician. And, of course, I didn't trust Julian one bit, especially after what Marlee had said about the facade he'd put up to hide his real emotions.

Even Melba wasn't quite off my suspect list, though I agreed with Marlee it would be foolish to murder someone before they could shell out a big sum of money.

"Not my murder to solve," I said under my breath.

"Are you talking to yourself?"

I sighed and turned around to see Euphoria standing on the sidewalk behind me. She had her arms crossed over her chest, and she was glaring at me. Her shoulders rose and fell rapidly, as if she were out of breath, and I wondered if she had hurried after me for some reason. Instead of answering her question, I said, "I hope the memorial goes well tonight."

I began to turn around so I could get into the hearse, but Euphoria's next words stopped me in my tracks.

"The next time you go tattling to Chief Constable Hightower about me, I will crush you."

CHAPTER FOURTEEN

ANGER AND FEAR ROSE in me in equal measure. My inner teenager was still afraid of Euphoria, but I was also angry that we were women in our fifties, and she was still resorting to threats and pettiness.

Euphoria was behaving like a child, but that didn't mean I had to stoop to her level. "I haven't done any tattling, about you or anyone else," I said calmly.

"I've spent years building a good relationship with Hightower." Euphoria took a step closer to me, and I wondered how I hadn't noticed the clack of her high heels on the sidewalk when she had rushed up behind me. "I've been trying to get on his good side since I was just a city councilwoman. You have no right to wreck all my hard work."

A new emotion began to churn in my chest. It wasn't quite anger. If I'd been forced to name it, I would have called it jealousy, though why I would feel jealous in that moment was beyond me.

I also felt betrayed. When I had told Wyatt about the conversation I'd heard between Euphoria and Julian, I had assumed it was in confidence. Had Wyatt repeated my report to the mayor? If so, then it was no wonder she was accusing me of tattling. I thought I had been helping out the constables, but Euphoria would see it as a personal attack.

Oh no, I thought wildly. *My magic is rising. Don't let it out. Don't let it out. Don't let it out.*

I crossed my arms, mirroring Euphoria's stance. Maybe, I thought, if I acted like I wasn't upset, then my magic wouldn't be as likely to build up and cause mayhem. "I haven't been trying to drive a wedge between you and Wyatt, if that's what you're implying."

"Someone told Hightower that Julian Ashcroft and I were happy about Fortie's murder," Euphoria said. "He didn't tell me who passed along that false tip, but I know it was you."

I felt a bit of relief at that. If nothing else, Wyatt hadn't betrayed my confidence, after all.

There was motion next to me, and I glanced over to see Marlee at my side. "Mayor, I had no idea you were psychic!"

Euphoria narrowed her eyes at Marlee. "I'm not psychic. I'm a witch. I did a Root Out the Rat spell. One of my own, of course. All I saw in my scrying mirror was pink, just like Hazel's lousy magic."

"Quite the leap," Marlee said, her voice chillingly calm.

My magic was still building, and I felt Marlee's arm snake through mine. To Euphoria, it would look like she was showing solidarity with me, but I knew she was doing it to help keep me calm.

Euphoria refused to back down. She looked at me again as she continued, "Hightower grilled me about my connection to Fortie and our history in Foxfire Haven's political scene, and he didn't trust me when I said I had an alibi for the night Fortie was killed. He wanted to know everything about our past disagreements on city matters, and he even implied that I was glad Fortie was dead. You even told him you thought I had killed him."

"As a matter of fact, I did not say that to Wyatt." Euphoria was definitely making a leap with that assumption, and the slight tinge of desperation in her tone made me feel a bit more relaxed. Either that, or Marlee's magic was working to balance out my own. "You just mentioned that you used to be on the city council. That means you and Fortie have a long history together. I'm sure the constables are talking to everyone in a similar situation. You're not being singled out, Euphoria."

The snarky side of me wanted to add, *So, maybe you're not as special as you think!* Thankfully, the more sensible part of my brain said no.

I should do a kindness spell tonight, I thought suddenly. *If I become as mean as Euphoria, then I'm no better than her. I don't want to be that person.*

Euphoria was retorting, but I wasn't even paying attention anymore. She seemed to realize her threats weren't going to get her anywhere, but she had one last barb for me. "If I find out you're trying to sabotage my career, it will end badly for you." With that, she spun on her shiny red high heel and went clacking away down the sidewalk.

I let out a breath, my shoulders sinking with relief. To my surprise, though, Marlee began to laugh. "What an immature bully!"

I reached out and pulled Marlee into a hug. "Thank you for coming to my rescue."

Marlee gave me a squeeze, then stepped back to peer at my face. "I was just about to pull away from the curb when I felt a wave of anxiety, and I knew it was coming from you. I got out of the car as fast as I could to come to your rescue, but I hadn't expected to find you going toe-to-toe with the mayor!"

"What did you expect?"

Marlee raised her arms to chest-height and curled her hands into fists. "I thought you might be squaring off with the killer!"

I laughed at that ridiculous mental image, and I felt myself calming further. Between Marlee's help and the diffusing of the situation with Euphoria, I was less worried that I'd have an uncontrolled magical exhalation right there on the sidewalk.

"Let's go home," I said. "Now I really want that pint of ice cream!"

Marlee insisted on walking me to the door of the hearse, and she stood on the sidewalk to keep an eye on me as I maneuvered out of my spot on the curb and onto the street.

When I got home, Marlee parked in the circular driveway while I guided the hearse around the side of the house. It had taken me a while to start using the detached garage in the backyard, because on my first visit to it, I'd found a dead body inside. But as the weeks had gone on and we'd gotten into drizzly late-fall weather, I'd become more concerned with keeping the hearse clean and dry than parking in a place where someone's body had been stashed.

By the time I had parked, shut and locked the garage door, then gone through the back door that led into the kitchen, Marlee had already pulled two bowls out of the cabinet. "We don't have mint-chip ice cream," she said as she fished two spoons from a drawer, "but I do have caramel chocolate crunch stashed in the back of the freezer."

"Sounds perfect," I enthused. I shrugged out of my coat, then hung it up on a hook by the door before making my way over to Perkins. He was asleep, his head tucked downward into the soft flannel nest. Lonnie, Valerian's raven, was perched on the radiator. "Keeping those toes warm, Lonnie?"

Lonnie cawed quietly in response, apparently not wanting to wake Perkins.

Marlee and I settled onto the couch in the living room with our bowls of ice cream. If any part of me had been interested in attending the memorial that night, my run-in with Euphoria had erased it. I didn't want to see her or Julian or anyone else that night, except my roommates.

Instead, Marlee and I put on a cheesy Christmas movie. It was a little early for such things since December had just begun, but it felt like the perfect complement to the ice cream.

"They should make Halloween movies like this," I commented. "A cute little romance set at a haunted house during a crisp October."

"Oh, I like it. Let's make it about a witch who falls in love with a non-magical person. We'll call it *Samhain Sweethearts*."

Marlee and I were so busy plotting our Halloween movie that we barely paid attention to what was on the screen. At one point, I nearly dropped my empty bowl because I was laughing so hard. It was exactly the silliness I needed after our memorable encounters downtown.

Once we'd come up with the happily-ever-after for our fictional movie couple, Marlee waved her spoon in the air. "We skipped right past dinner. You hungry?"

"We should probably eat something a bit healthier than this. Otherwise, we won't be strong enough to strut down the red carpet at our movie premiere." I volunteered to make a quick stir-fry with some left-overs, and before long, Marlee and I were sitting down at the breakfast nook to eat.

We were only halfway through when Marlee's phone buzzed. She had set the phone on the table, and she glanced lazily at the screen. Then, she dropped her fork onto her plate and sat up straighter. "Oh no!"

"What's wrong?" I leaned forward, trying to see the text message.

"A friend of mine from book club broke down driving back from Stanton. She said the tow truck can't get there for two hours! She's asking me to pick her up."

I relaxed, realizing Marlee's initial distress had probably been some of her empathy magic. She had momentarily felt her friend's emotions about being broken down on the side of the road during a cold, dark night. "Want me to go with you? That way, you won't have to drive alone on the way there."

Marlee's fingers had been flying across the screen of her phone while she responded to her friend, and after a moment's pause, she looked up at me. "No need. Her car is only three miles outside of town. But I'd appreciate it if you could put the rest of my dinner in the fridge. I'll finish up when I get back."

"You got it."

Two minutes later, I had seen Marlee out the front door, and I was alone in the house. I put Marlee's dinner into a container and stashed it in the fridge, then scarfed down the rest of mine. By the time I had cleaned up, I had made up my mind to use the time to myself to do a kindness spell. There wasn't one in my grimoire, but I figured I could come up with something fairly easily.

I collected some dried bluebell, a small piece of jade, and a light-blue candle from the bookshelf in my bedroom. There were only a few actual books on it, since most of the shelves held my growing collection of items for working magic. I had returned to Foxfire Haven with just a handful of magical things, but I was quickly rectifying that.

As I gathered the items, I tried out some different incantations about kindness. One of them rhymed, and another was so long I forgot it as soon as I'd said it. I was on my fifth or sixth try when I landed on a phrase that felt light and uplifting.

I arranged my items for the spell on the kitchen table, then turned off the overhead light. I had to stand by the light switch for a moment as my eyes adjusted to the darkness, but before long, the glow from the back-porch light filtering through the linen curtains gave me enough illumination to see what I was doing. I made my way to the table and sat down, all while reminding myself that I was completely capable of working magic on my own.

Actually, the thought I had was that I could practice witchcraft without adult supervision. I was still working on regaining my confidence as a witch, but I figured there was little that could go wrong with a kindness spell.

Right?

Confidence spells could backfire, as I'd learned the hard way. Thankfully, our coven had performed that one in the backyard, so when my magic had built up as my confidence soared, the resulting release of it had only tipped over a porch chair. And one of my roommates.

An amplification spell I'd tried on my own had ended with similar results.

I shook my head, trying to get those kinds of thoughts out of my mind. Starting a spell with a doubtful heart was never a good idea. "I can do this," I told myself.

Perkins must have sensed my hesitance, because he roused himself from his nest and flew to the table. He scooted close to my left arm and nuzzled against me. As he did, I felt a wave of gentle confidence.

"Thanks, Perky. You're always kind, aren't you? You don't need a spell to be sweet."

I lit the candle and began to repeat the phrase I'd decided on for my incantation. After I'd said it three times, I lifted the bluebell bundle. "I use bluebell to aid my magic, a flower that resonates with kindness and love." I then said the incantation another three times before lifting the piece of jade. "I use jade to aid my—"

A sharp tapping against the kitchen window nearest the table startled me, and I looked up to see Lonnie peering at me from the other side of the pane, her head tilted and her black beak silhouetted against the night sky.

Lonnie jerked her head three times in the direction of the street, then tapped her beak against the window again. The raven wasn't my familiar, so I didn't have the ability to understand her the way Valerian could, but I instantly knew something was wrong, and she wanted me to go outside to help.

"On my way," I shouted. I blew out the candle as I stood, the chair nearly falling over in my haste, and dashed toward the front door.

CHAPTER FIFTEEN

PERKINS WAS OUT OF the house before I was. As soon as I'd announced to Lonnie that I was on my way, Perkins had swooped out the window that looked out over the back porch. We always kept it open just enough for our flying familiars to come and go.

Lonnie and Perkins were both circling the air near the front door, and as I rushed out of it, Lonnie led the way down the driveway. When we reached the street, she careened left and quickly outpaced Perkins.

"It's okay, Perky," I said breathlessly as I hustled along. "I can't keep up with her, either."

Thankfully, we didn't have far to go. There was a wooded area between two of the houses a short distance down the street, and I saw Lonnie there, circling again in the shine of a streetlamp. Every now and then, she would dive lower, then rise up again.

As I got closer, I began to hear a noise that was unmistakable. A cat was in distress. The cacophony of howling and hissing was mixed with the sound of dull thuds. I instantly thought of Wyatt's cat, Jazz. The hulking black cat was the nemesis of our familiars. I'd first met Wyatt when Jazz had attacked Perkins, and I decided to lecture the cat's owner about it rather than the cat himself.

"Has Jazz been mean to one of you?" I asked as I came to a stop at the edge of the wooded area. Lonnie, of course, couldn't answer, but she did swoop down again, finally coming to rest on a fallen tree branch.

I heard light but rapid footsteps nearby, and I looked up to see Wyatt running toward me from the direction of his house. Unlike me, he wasn't out of breath at all. "What have your birds done to my cat now?"

"What has your cat done to our birds?" I countered.

Wyatt and I turned toward the sound of Jazz's continued cries to find out exactly that. Except, when I looked, I didn't see the cat. Wyatt took two steps forward, stepping carefully over the small plants and fallen branches at the edge of the wooded area. He held out an arm to bar my way. "Stay there. I don't want you to trip over something in the dark."

"Over there," I said, pointing to a spot slightly to our right. "I think Jazz is inside that crate." The square shape was barely visible, since it was half-covered by trailing English ivy. It sat right at the edge of the streetlamp's glow, and the only reason I had looked in that direction was because both Gordon and Stella were flying low circles over the spot.

As we watched, Gordon landed on the ground next to the crate and began to push against it with his huge beak. He looked from the crate to Wyatt, then back to the crate.

"They're trying to help him," I said.

Wyatt stepped carefully, and when he got close to the crate, Gordon and Stella moved away to give him space.

"Someone dumped an old wooden bin out here," Wyatt grumbled. "I thought we had nicer neighbors than that."

"With all that ivy growing over it, I'm guessing it's been there for a while."

"Probably." The hissing and yowling ceased as Wyatt lifted one corner of the crate, and Jazz shot out of it. He ran a short distance away, then turned back and began to weave between Wyatt's legs. Wyatt bent down and scratched Jazz's head. "You okay, big guy?"

"He must have wiggled his way under the edge of the bin, then he couldn't get out," I speculated. "Lonnie—that's the raven—came and tapped on my window to let me know Jazz was in trouble."

Wyatt stood up straight and looked at the birds, who had settled in a line on the biggest of the fallen branches. "How about that? Why would they help when they were trying to hurt Jazz not long ago?"

"They never tried to hurt Jazz. He's the one who cornered Perkins, and all the birds did was warn Jazz off the next time he came slinking around." I was fighting not to let an edge of resentment into my voice. The birds had never wanted to harm the cat. They had just stood up to him to let him know they wouldn't put up with his intimidation. "That was two months ago, and Jazz has left them alone since then. I guess the birds repaid him by helping out when he needed it."

Such kind birds, I thought. They were willing to help out, regardless of how Jazz had treated them in the past.

That reminded me of my kindness spell. I hadn't been able to finish it, but it was ironic that the interruption had come because the birds were doing something kind.

And I should be putting kindness into practice, too.
"Do you want to come back to the house for a cup of
tea?" I asked abruptly, before I could change my mind.
"I'm sure you're under a lot of stress and working crazy
hours because of Fortie's murder investigation."

Wyatt hesitated, then looked down at Jazz. "I should
probably get Jazz home and make sure he's okay."

The cat was clearly fine. He was happily rubbing
against one of Wyatt's legs.

"Bring him along. I think he knows to behave himself."

Wyatt didn't give his usual grunt. Instead, it was a
softer version that showed he was still debating whether
to take me up on the offer.

"Marlee brought home cookies from a tasting session
for a wedding client," I added. I really wanted this win,
and I suddenly realized I was trying to push my kindness
on someone who might not want it. "But, of course, I
understand if you'd rather head home."

"Did Karla from The Salt Circle bake them?"

"Yeah. Marlee usually goes to her for wedding cakes
and other baked items she needs for events."

"Okay, then. That sounds good."

We must have looked utterly ridiculous as we walked
to the funeral home. Gordon and Lonnie led the way,
flying just a few feet higher than Wyatt's head. Jazz followed, his tail sticking straight up as he trotted along.
Perkins had settled onto my shoulder, and Stella was
flying next to Wyatt and me, though she was keeping
her distance. The shy toucan hadn't quite warmed up to
Wyatt yet.

When we reached my driveway, I realized I'd left the
front door wide open in my haste.

Or had I? Had the door opened of its own accord again? I couldn't remember whether I'd slammed it shut behind me or not.

"Good thing our town is pretty safe," Wyatt commented as we walked up the driveway.

"I guess I was in too much of a hurry to find out what the emergency was," I answered. There was no reason to explain that there was possibly a second ghost haunting the old funeral home, and that it might be the one opening the door.

I led the way to the kitchen and gestured toward one of the chairs at the table in the breakfast nook. "Have a seat. I'll put the kettle on." As Wyatt moved to comply, I hastily swept the items I'd arranged for my kindness spell to one side.

Jazz had hesitated at the front door, but after a few reassuring words from Wyatt, he had followed. As I filled the tea kettle with water, I saw Jazz hop up onto Wyatt's lap and curl into a ball.

"I'm glad he's okay," I said.

"Me, too. Jazz is usually good about staying out of trouble. Despite what you think, he's a good cat."

"I realize cats and birds aren't usually the best of friends," I admitted. "But I'm sure you understand that I'm a bit protective of Perky."

"Perky?"

I nodded toward my owl, who was busy finding a comfortable position in his flannel nest. "I've had Perkins since I was thirteen. The toucan next to him is Stella, Marlee's familiar."

"The raven is Valerian's. I saw her at the tavern once." Wyatt nodded toward Gordon, who was standing in one corner of the room, slowly looking from side to side, as if he were guarding the kitchen. "That means the pelican belongs to Josephine."

"Jo, yes."

"You've got quite the group of witches living here."

I couldn't tell if Wyatt was trying to pay a compliment or criticize us. Or, perhaps, he was simply trying to make conversation. I decided to take his comment as a way to keep us from lapsing into silence, and I explained how grateful I was to have found such supportive, accepting women to rent the rooms. As I spoke, I spooned dried chamomile and spearmint into the teapot and pulled two delicate teacups out of the cabinet.

By the time I had poured the hot water into the teapot and laid a plate of almond cookies onto the table, I realized it was the longest conversation Wyatt and I had ever had. It was slightly awkward, and I knew we were both treading carefully so we wouldn't stray into our usual sharpness with each other, but it still felt good to have a semi-normal moment with the man.

As I sat down opposite Wyatt, I said, "I would have expected you to attend the memorial for Fortie tonight."

"A few of the other constables are there to represent the department." Wyatt bit into a cookie, his expression smoothing into one of contentedness. After he swallowed, he added, "I never liked Fortie that much anyway. I'm surprised you're not there, trying to pin down suspects."

I looked up from pouring the tea just in time to see the teasing glint in Wyatt's eyes. He had a sense of humor, after all. "No way was I going to risk running into Euphoria again."

"What's the story with you two? She talks about you like you're a plague on this town."

I absently ran a fingertip around the scalloped edge of my teacup while I considered how honest I should be with Wyatt. It didn't take me long to decide to be totally transparent with him. I wasn't sure why I was trusting him with something that felt so personal, but in the moment, it seemed like the right choice. "We were in the same grade in school," I began. "I never really fit in here. I mean, I had a few close friends, but I was never one of the popular kids."

"Unlike Euphoria."

"Exactly. I wasn't that strong of a witch. I'm still not, as you well know. And I wasn't pretty enough or charismatic enough to make up for it. I was really self-conscious back then, and Euphoria knew it. She bullied me, always cutting me down and making me feel like I was useless."

"That's not an easy thing to let go of," Wyatt said. I could hear the sympathy in his tone.

"No, it's not. When I moved back here, I ran into Euphoria, and she's still determined to be awful to me. It doesn't get to me like it did when I was a teenager, but it's still really tiring. I don't know why she's hung onto that bad attitude all these years."

"Because she never grew up, like you did." Wyatt picked up his teacup, which looked tiny in his hand. "She's used her intimidation and bullying to get her all the way to city mayor, but as her status has improved, her attitude hasn't."

I could have hugged Wyatt for saying that. It felt good to have someone else acknowledge what I'd already observed.

"I had a run-in with her today." I reached out and picked up the jade, then rolled it between my fingers. "I was doing a spell to be more kind to people like her when Lonnie alerted me to Jazz's emergency."

Wyatt eyed the assortment of items I'd gathered for my spell. "It doesn't seem like you should need magic to be nice to someone."

"You were never bullied by Euphoria!" I gave a short laugh. "But, you're right. The spell isn't about needing magic to change how I treat people. Sometimes, the act of doing a spell or ritual is a way to keep your goal in focus, so you'll be more mindful of it. Magic is a tool, not a solution."

Wyatt smiled into his teacup. "Constance used to say the same thing," he said quietly.

"Who's Constance?"

CHAPTER SIXTEEN

WYATT'S BODY STIFFENED, AND his smile turned into a tightlipped frown. He had clearly said something he hadn't meant to. He picked up another cookie as he shifted in his chair. "Constance was my wife. My late wife." He took a massive bite of the cookie and stared out the window.

"My condolences." Valerian had once mentioned Wyatt had been married at one point, but she hadn't been sure what had happened. Now I knew her name had been Constance, and she had died. And, since she had shared a similar view as me about magic's usefulness, then she had likely been a witch, too.

"It was years ago," Wyatt said around a mouthful of cookie. He swallowed, then took a swig of tea. "Well, thanks for the tea. I should get Jazz home. He's worn out after his adventure." Wyatt scooped Jazz off his lap and gently put the cat on the ground.

"I'll walk you to the door," I said. Wyatt was moving so quickly, though, that I wound up trailing after him as he saw himself out.

I stood in the open doorway and waited as Wyatt and Jazz walked down the driveway. When they reached the street, I shut the door, afraid Wyatt might look over his shoulder and catch me watching.

Slowly, I returned to the kitchen and began to clear the table. "What a strange evening," I commented to Perkins. He opened one eye and gave a low hoot.

Once the tea and cookies had been taken care of, I gathered the items for the kindness spell and put them in a small basket sitting nearby. I was too tired to make another attempt at the spell that night.

I had hoped I would have kindness on my mind when I went to bed, because I knew it would be a good frame of mind to be in as I drifted off to sleep. Instead, I found myself constantly coming back to the same question: what had happened to Constance, and why was Wyatt so uncomfortable talking about her if she had died years ago, as he'd said?

At least I didn't wake up on Wednesday morning still thinking about Wyatt and his late wife. Instead, I opened my eyes and realized I had my mystery client's pickup and delivery that day. *Maybe,* I told myself as I got dressed, *Wyatt simply likes his privacy, just like this client does.*

Okay, so I hadn't woken up thinking about Wyatt, but he was in my thoughts approximately four minutes and twenty-five seconds after climbing out of bed.

Ugh.

I was scheduled to arrive at the client's house at ten o'clock, so I had a fairly leisurely morning before it was time to head out. The street name the client had given me wasn't one I recognized, and I was grateful for the map function on my cell phone. Otherwise, I would have had to break out one of Uncle Grant's old paper maps of Foxfire Haven.

The address was farther outside of town than I had expected, but before long, I was guiding the hearse along a narrow two-lane road that wound up and down steep hills. I nearly missed the turnoff for the street my client lived on because it was a dirt road barely wide enough for one vehicle. The speedometer read fifteen miles per hour as I drove down it, and even that felt too fast. The trees seemed entirely too close for comfort, especially when I was trying to keep such a massive vehicle in the center of the road.

The narrow road made a long, lazy bend to the left, and at the end of it, I drove into an open space with a gorgeous two-story log cabin sitting in the middle of it. Both sides of the cabin had gardens that grew right up to the walls, but there was nothing orderly about the plants. The gardens looked almost wild, like they had just sprung up naturally. The fuchsias and asters would make the place look spectacular in the spring and summer.

There was a small stack of boxes on the wide covered front porch, and I pulled up in front of the cabin so the back of the hearse was close to the porch steps. As the client had promised, there was a white envelope on top of a box, held in place with a rock. Inside the envelope, I found cash and the address of the thrift store in Stanton where I'd be delivering the boxes.

I opened the rear door of the hearse and began to load up the boxes. As I did so, I spared some looks around me to further appreciate what a beautiful spot the cabin was in. The tall fir trees pressed in all around it, but rather than feeling claustrophobic, the trees gave me the sense that they were standing guard. I felt protected, like the cabin was in a little bubble that was somehow separate from the rest of the world.

It felt magical, but it was a different kind of magic than mine. This was something far more ancient, a mystical piece of the natural world.

I was tempted to take a break and sit down in one of the rocking chairs on the front porch. In my mind, I pictured myself rocking back and forth slowly, a pleasant breeze making the flowers sway gently while bees buzzed past, hard at work. This, I decided, would be the perfect place to spend a warm spring day.

Instead, though, it was winter, and I was there to do a job. There would be no lazy rocking for me. With a sigh, I continued loading up.

Everything was easy to get into the back of the hearse, until I reached the last item in the pile. It wasn't a cardboard box but an antique desk chair. The arms and legs were solid wood, with a floral design carved into them. The seat was upholstered in a midnight-blue velvet. It looked just as comfortable as the rocking chairs on the front porch.

Unfortunately for me, the chair was as heavy as it was beautiful. It was on wheels, so I could easily roll it to the edge of the porch, but I couldn't get it down the steps, let alone into the hearse. After a few attempts to hoist it up, I finally gave up with a groan. My shoulders and back were not happy about the unexpected workout.

I descended the steps, then turned around to gaze at the chair. Maybe, I thought, I could rig up some kind of ramp to get it onto the ground, then use that same ramp to get the chair into the hearse. Nothing in the immediate vicinity caught my eye, though, so I sighed and decided to give it another try.

This time, I did manage to get all four legs of the chair off the ground, but I overcompensated for the weight by leaning back too far. I dropped the chair, which clattered to the porch floorboards while I stumbled backward. I managed to stop my momentum just before tottering right off the edge of the porch.

"Wait. I'll help."

I jumped at the unexpected voice, and for the second time, I very nearly tumbled down the steps. It was the same voice I'd heard on the phone, and I still couldn't quite place who it belonged to.

Before turning to see who was talking, I took one long stride away from the porch steps. It seemed like the safe thing to do. Then, I turned slowly in the direction of the voice. It was a good thing I had moved, because I jumped again, but this time, I wasn't in danger of pitching right off the porch.

It wasn't a human standing near the front of the hearse. It was a Bigfoot. Barry, to be exact. He had to be more than seven feet tall, and his honey-colored fur shimmered in the sunlight that was peeking out from the clouds.

"I knew I recognized your voice when you called," I said. My own voice was shaking. I wasn't scared of Barry. Rather, I was on high alert after nearly falling.

"I should have realized the chair would be too heavy for you."

"I'm sorry I ruined your attempt at being anonymous with my weak little arms." To drive home my point, I squeezed a thumb and forefinger around my upper arm.

Barry shrugged. "It's okay. I went for a walk in the woods, and I just got back." He glanced toward a trail leading into the trees, then looked at me again. "I thought you might be done already."

At least he wasn't standing in the woods, spying on me having a fight with a chair.

Despite his size, Barry was surprisingly graceful. He loped forward and joined me on the porch in just three strides. It was only then I realized the cabin must have been specially built for him, because the roof overhead was tall enough to accommodate him easily.

"This is a beautiful home," I said.

Barry's eyes, which were only a slightly darker golden shade than his fur, lit up. "Thank you. I did a lot of the work myself, and I'm very happy with how it turned out." He reached out and easily lifted the chair with one arm, and within seconds, he'd gotten it loaded inside the hearse.

"You make it look so easy," I commented as I swung the door shut. "I know this is a nosy question, but I'm just taking some of your old things to the thrift store. Why do you care about anyone finding out about that?"

Barry reached up and ran a hand through the fur on top of his head. He'd brightened when talking about his cabin, but the downtrodden look he always had at the tavern had returned instantly when I asked my question. "Because it's not just my old belongings. I bought a few things to have around the house because I knew my girlfriend would enjoy them. We broke up a while back, and I couldn't take the reminders of her anymore. I just...didn't want anyone gossiping about it."

Without thinking, I laid a hand on Barry's arm. His fur was silky soft, and I had to resist the urge to run my fingers across it. *He's a person, not a dog,* I lectured myself. "I totally understand. We all have events in our lives that we don't want the whole town talking about."

"You sound like you're speaking from experience."

"I'll tell you what. The next time you and I are both at the tavern, and I have a drink in my hand, I'll tell you about my big, fat magical secret that I don't want anyone in Foxfire Haven to find out about." I squeezed Barry's arm before dropping my hand and adding gently, "You should know, though, that you looking so forlorn at the tavern all the time is kind of a dead giveaway that you're going through something."

"Oh, that's not just about the breakup. But Val never presses for details."

"She's good about giving people their space."

Barry growled quietly. "Unlike Melba Hawthorn. People at the tavern leave me alone, which is one of the reasons I'm there so often. Melba used to come past my cabin all the time while she was out hiking and collecting herbs, and she's the biggest busybody in this town. I'd go to the tavern just to get away from her. My luck must be changing, though, because I haven't seen her since last week."

CHAPTER SEVENTEEN

"MELBA USED TO BE here a lot?" I asked.

"She claimed it was because there's a great patch of wild lavender nearby, but I know it was because she wanted to pry into my business." Barry wrinkled his nose. "Melba would always tell me that for a fee, she'd be happy to help with whatever was bothering me. But I haven't seen her since Friday morning."

"The same day Fortie was killed," I pointed out.

Barry gave me a sidelong glance. "I'm not sure what that has to do with it."

"Apparently, it's no secret Fortie had been going to Melba for magical help. Most recently, he was using her services to try to avoid his fate. I went to her website to book a consultation with her, just out of curiosity, but she had no openings for the next three weeks."

"Which means she hasn't had time to be out hiking and harassing me. Business must have been slow before, but now she's slammed."

"Exactly. Fortie's death has been really good for Melba's business, probably because of people like me who are curious to know about the woman who failed to prevent his demise."

Barry began to laugh, a deep, rumbling sound that echoed in the clearing in front of the cabin. "I've heard Val talking about how clever you are. She was really impressed with the way you put the pieces together to solve Steve Zillmann's murder. She also said it was fun to watch you do it, and she was right."

I felt heat in my cheeks from the unexpected praise. "I haven't figured out this one yet," I countered. "Besides, Fortie wasn't ditched in my garage, like Steve was. I'm sitting back and letting the constables figure out who killed Fortie."

"Sure you are." Barry, clearly, wasn't buying it for a heartbeat.

And, of course, he was right not to believe me. I hadn't yet discounted Melba as a suspect, and with the knowledge that she'd had lots of free time, right up until Fortie's death, I had to wonder, again, if she'd had something to do with it. Maybe she'd expected her star to rise in the wake of his murder. She would never get the money from Fortie's birthday ritual, but she'd more than make up for that with all the curious new clients she'd get.

That, though, was something I could ponder later. Right then, I had a job to finish up. I said goodbye to Barry, promising again that I wouldn't breathe a word about him or his donated items to anyone.

As I made the thirty-minute drive to the thrift store in Stanton, I realized that had been only the second time I'd ever talked to Barry, despite seeing him often at the tavern. He had been friends with Uncle Grant, and my conversation with him today had shown me why Grant would have liked him. Barry was smart and kind, and I wished him all the best as he tried to get over his breakup.

A couple of employees at the thrift store had to assist me in unloading the chair. As two men pulled it out of the back of the hearse, something fluttered onto the ground. It looked like a scrap of paper that had gotten wedged between one of the arms and the upholstered seat. Quickly, I snatched it up, just in case it had any of Barry's personal information on it.

It didn't. It looked like part of a page torn from a notebook, and the only words written on it read *spectacular view*. I crumpled up the paper and shoved it into the pocket of my jeans so I could throw it away later.

On the drive back to Foxfire Haven, I pondered the sudden uptick in business for both Melba and Gemma. The two witches had suddenly become the most sought-after consultants in town, and my curiosity to meet both women was still strong.

First, though, I had my own magical consultation to perform. I had a lunchtime video call scheduled with Hailey.

As soon as I got back to the funeral home, I grabbed some leftovers out of the fridge and ate them right out of the container. Cold lasagna was not my idea of a good lunch, but time was short.

Is there a spell for rapidly reheating food? I wondered. "If microwaves can be considered magical," I muttered.

Soon, I was looking at Hailey's dimpled smile and excited gray eyes on the screen of my phone. Tara was bent down, looking at me over Hailey's shoulder. "She hasn't wrecked any other electronics since we last spoke," Tara said.

"That's good. Have you had any other incidents?"

Tara bit her lip as her eyes slid downward toward her daughter. "Hailey, honey, why don't you go get that painting you made? I'm sure Grandma would love to see it."

"Okay!" Hailey disappeared from sight.

As soon as she was gone, Tara said quietly, "She told a little boy at preschool that if he didn't let her play with his toy, she'd turn him into a fish."

"And she admitted that to you?"

"No. The boy told the teacher, and she reported it to us. Of course, she doesn't know Hailey might actually give the kid gills."

I shook my head. "No. Witchcraft isn't quite that dramatic. But during our lesson today, I'll reiterate the need to practice magic kindly."

Maybe I'll be teaching Hailey a spell today. She could benefit from the kindness spell.

We would, of course, skip the part where she would need to light a candle. I wasn't about to trust a three-year-old witch with fire.

Hailey returned soon, a piece of green construction paper clutched in her hand. She'd covered most of one side with finger paint, and I politely asked her to describe the scene to me, since I had no idea what it was and didn't want to admit it.

After Hailey said it was a depiction of her cat, we moved on to our usual lessons to help her contain her magic. It was a fun hour, but by the end of it, she was yawning, and so was I.

I ended the call after teaching Hailey a simpler version of the kindness incantation, and then I headed straight for my bedroom so I could squeeze in a quick nap before I went to Gemma's with the rest of my coven.

By the time I'd woken up and gotten ready for our outing, the rest of my roommates were home. I found Jo and Valerian in the living room, chatting about tavern gossip. Marlee was at the kitchen table, which she had covered with calendar pages. She explained she was trying to plan a timeline for a new client who wanted a lavish wedding in just eight weeks.

Marlee was the only one who grumbled about heading to Gemma's, but I knew that was only because she was feeling stressed about the wedding. "Maybe," I told her, "Gemma will have some insight about that."

That perked Marlee right up, and soon, the four of us were piled into her compact SUV.

"Coven outing!" Jo said in a singsong tone as Marlee drove us toward Gemma's.

"I think this is the first time we've gone out as a group to somewhere that wasn't the tavern or a restaurant," Valerian pointed out. "We should do more things like this. It's good for continuing our bonding as a coven."

"And better for our health." Marlee reached over and patted the bag of frozen peas Jo had placed on the center console. "This food is going to tell our futures rather than expand our waistlines."

When we arrived at Gemma's house, Marlee quickly found a parking space a short way down the street. Not only was it easier to park than our previous attempt, but the line in front of the house was shorter, too. Only three people were lined up along the walk.

"Is Gemma's burst of business on the wane already?" Valerian mused as we joined the queue.

"It's earlier now than the last time we were here," Marlee pointed out. "I expect we've beaten the work crowd."

As if to prove her point, two more people walked up just then and got in line behind us. By the time we were next in line, another three people had arrived.

The customers who came out of Gemma's front door after their reading weren't as exuberant as the man we'd seen the first time. They were either more sedate about their futures, or they hadn't gotten anything quite as dramatic as the news they were going to live a long life.

Finally, it was our turn. The woman who'd been in line ahead of us came out of the house, gave us an encouraging smile, and told us to head on inside.

The front door opened onto a small entryway, where we quickly shed our coats before moving into a long hallway. On the left was a living room decorated in what I thought of as stereotypical witch style. There were shelves containing old leather-bound books and jars of who-knew-what. The coffee table held a bowl filled with some kind of dried herb, and there were candles on nearly every available surface.

"Come in, ladies."

I turned to see Gemma standing in the doorway to the right, opposite the living room. She was wearing a long blue dress, which she had accented with about ten silver necklaces and a knitted gold scarf that hung in one long loop from her neck.

"I see you brought your own peas. Good, good." Gemma motioned for us to follow her, and I noticed she wasn't using a cane, like she had at the farmers market. Either she only needed it for walking longer distances, or it was a way to look more dramatic when she was out in public. "I've hardly got any left. I need to get to the store for more, but people keep showing up to learn their fates."

The room Gemma led us into was a dining room. She had pulled the heavy green velvet curtains closed, completely shutting out the late-afternoon daylight. The only light came from candles burning in a tray on the dark wooden floor and a string of small white lights that ran around the top of the walls.

In a normal dining room, the table would be in the middle, surrounded by chairs. Here, though, the table had been shoved against one wall, and the six chairs were positioned in a circle around the tray of candles. Gemma invited us all to sit as she took the bag of frozen peas from Jo's hand.

Once we were settled into our chairs, Gemma walked a slow circle in front of us, pausing to stare at each of our faces. Marlee giggled uncomfortably when Gemma bent down close to inspect her, and Valerian leaned so far back I worried her chair would topple right over.

I didn't do much better. I tried to hold Gemma's intense gaze, but I soon had to avert my eyes.

Once she was done inspecting us, or reading our souls, or whatever she was doing, Gemma cut open the bag of peas, her scissors flashing in the candlelight, and proceeded to dump the entire contents onto the floor. She stretched out the arm holding the bag and moved it in a wide circle so the peas fell all around the tray of candles.

Once the last *tink* of a frozen pea hitting the wooden floor had sounded, Gemma clapped her hands. "Now! Let's see what lies in store for each of you."

Gemma slowly waved her arms over the peas closest to Jo, her bent fingers moving slowly, almost as if she were typing. "You made a decision about your future recently," she told Jo. "Don't second-guess yourself. You chose wisely."

Jo's mouth fell open, and she nodded slowly.

Gemma squeezed between Jo and the peas to focus on what she saw in front of Marlee. "Oh. Oh. Yes." Gemma smiled sweetly at Marlee. "You've been waiting a long time, but don't worry. Your turn is coming."

Marlee looked surprised, then confused. She opened her mouth to speak, but Gemma was already sliding in front of Valerian, her fingers still moving over the peas.

"You know about flavors. What tastes good, and what doesn't." Gemma raised a finger and pointed it toward Valerian. "Life is a lot like your potions. It's easier to catch flies with honey."

It was hard to tell in the dim light, but I thought I saw Valerian roll her eyes once Gemma had turned away from her.

It was my turn next. Gemma had barely looked at the peas in front of me when she curled her hands into fists and yanked her arms close to her chest. "I see murder!"

CHAPTER EIGHTEEN

"I'M GOING TO BE murdered?" I blurted. My eyes darted to the floor, looking from one group of peas to the next. I didn't see anything that looked like murder. I just saw a bunch of frozen peas.

"No," Gemma said calmly. "But I see murder around you. You're involved."

I let out a relieved laugh. "I assure you, I'm not planning to murder anyone. It must be a mistake."

"You've been involved in Fortie's murder investigation," Valerian pointed out.

"Oh. That's true."

"I predicted it!" Gemma said, her voice nearly rising to a shout. "I knew he was going to die."

"I understand you saw Fortie's demise a while back, and he was working with Melba to stay alive," I prompted, eager for more details.

"Yes. I told him Melba charges too much money, but Fortie had been going to her for years, looking for help with this and that. Of course, I can't begrudge her the money. Goodness knows she needs it."

I thought back to what Barry had said about Melba walking through the woods near him so often, and my speculation that she'd had a lot of free time on her hands. "Was her business not doing well?"

"That I don't know. I just know she's trying to buy a big tract of land next to her house, so some greedy soul doesn't get it and build a fast-food restaurant on it."

"How likely is that?" Valerian wondered. "This isn't the kind of town developers are clamoring to build chain stores in."

Gemma shrugged. "Who knows? I told Melba to come to me, and I'd be able to give her some insight about the situation, but oh, no, she said she didn't need my help. She thinks she can get all the answers through her own witchcraft, but sometimes, you need outside help."

"Like the members of your coven," Marlee said.

"Or someone skilled at divining the future," Gemma countered, sounding mildly offended.

"It would have been smart for Melba to consult with you," Jo said quickly. "We're certainly glad we did, because you've given us a lot to think about."

Gemma smiled, placated by the praise. "I'm happy to hear it. Now, if you'll excuse me, I'm going to check the line outside and grab the broom. You ladies sit tight."

After Gemma had left the room, Jo said, "You know, I think I heard about that land. If Melba's home is where I think it is, then the land is a beautiful patch of forested area. It's up for sale, and it's zoned for residential and commercial. It's out on the edge of town, so honestly, it wouldn't have much effect on any of us if it gets turned into a fast-food place, roller-skating rink, or any other thing."

"It would have a big effect on Melba," Valerian pointed out. "Even if the land is on the outskirts of town, I think it should stay forested. It creates a nice, natural barrier between Foxfire Haven and the highway."

I used the highway to shuttle deliveries to and from places like Stanton, and it was a lot busier than the two-lane road that led in to and out of Foxfire Haven. Already, businesses had cropped up where the highway and the road into town met. I, for one, was grateful for the coffee shop there, so I could grab something to go before making the drive to Stanton.

At the same time, I didn't want to roll past a line of generic, non-magical places on my way into Foxfire Haven.

"I can see why Melba would want to prevent the land from being developed, either for houses or businesses," I said. "Apparently, she likes walking through the woods a lot." And, I realized, her house and Barry's probably weren't too far from each other. I was certain he'd prefer the land remain forested, too.

"Hazel!" Marlee's face looked comically shocked in the flicker of the candles. "You've been looking into Melba as a suspect in Fortie's murder, haven't you?"

I laughed. "Did you jump to that conclusion because I said she likes hiking or because you felt my suspicions rolling off me?"

"Both. You've never met the woman, so when you throw out a tidbit like that, I know you've been looking into her."

"It wasn't on purpose. I had a delivery to make today, and the client mentioned running into Melba on a regular basis because she's always wandering through the nearby woods. At least, she was, right up until Fortie was murdered. Now, she's booked solid, so she hasn't been on her walks this week."

"I didn't know you had a delivery run this morning," Valerian said. "Who was it for?"

I was grateful for the dim lighting because it meant my coven couldn't see how awkward I felt in that moment. I was sure my cheeks were flushing, and I resisted the urge to scoot backward in my chair. "Um, the client asked to remain anonymous because of some personal stuff."

"Smart move," Valerian said. "That's how you keep from becoming town gossip."

My body relaxed as I saw Marlee and Jo nod in agreement. I had expected some pushback, but all three of them seemed to recognize that some people simply wanted privacy.

Gemma came back into the room, an old wooden broom in her hand. As she began to sweep the peas into a pile, Marlee asked, "What do you do with all these peas after a reading?"

"I feed them to my chickens out back. They're eating like kings right now! A few of them had been doing poorly lately, but they're perking up nicely."

"Gemma," I said, "Newton Yates said you foresaw death for him, too, but now his future is looking good. How does that work?"

Gemma paused her sweeping and gave me a knowing look. "Our futures aren't set in stone. Newton made choices that altered his. Though, I've also wondered if the death prediction I got during Newton's reading wasn't actually a message about Fortie. Newton said the peas he brought in that day had come from Fortie's freezer." Gemma lifted the hand not holding the broom and waggled her fingers. "It's possible they were tainted with Fortie's energy."

In that case, I realized, every prediction Gemma had made for us could have actually been about Jo, since she was the one who had bought the peas and carried them to our reading.

Is there really any magic to predictions like this, or is it all guesswork?

Either way, we still had to pay. Gemma only accepted cash, and we all dug into our purses to pull out the required fee. We were told there were no group discounts, though we did get the promised price break for bringing our own peas.

The drive back to the funeral home was a lively one. I was a bit disappointed in my prediction, and I didn't waste any time telling my roommates how I felt. Since I was already involved in Fortie's murder investigation, the news that Gemma saw murder in my future was so in line with my present that it hadn't been a true revelation.

Valerian wasn't thrilled with her reading, either. "All Gemma did was tell me to be a nicer person. I'm nice enough. My patrons tip me well, and even though I can be a bit rough around the edges sometimes, it doesn't mean I need to go changing my personality. Being straightforward is a good thing."

"We like you just as you are," Marlee reassured Valerian. "Even when you're fussing about patrons who need to stop complaining to you about all their problems."

"I do not fuss."

The rest of us burst out laughing. Valerian was constantly telling us about someone who'd come to the bar for a beer and wound up pouring their heart out to her.

She referred to bartending as being a therapist, but with alcohol. She liked to complain about her role, but we all knew she enjoyed it deep down.

"I liked my prediction, though I'm not sure what it could have meant," Marlee said. "I've been waiting a long time for my business to be successful enough that I can afford to hire an assistant, so maybe it was about that. At the same time, I'm fifty-four years old, and I've never been married."

"I do not recommend it," Valerian said. She barked out a laugh, then added, "Oh, Gemma is right. I do need to be nicer."

"Anyway," Marlee said, ignoring Valerian's comment, "I wonder if she means my turn to be married is coming soon."

"Ooh," we all chorused.

We were debating whether Marlee should handle the planning for her own wedding or let us do it for her as we pulled into the driveway. The headlights of Marlee's SUV swept across the front porch, and we saw a man standing there. He had a black wool coat pulled close around his robust body.

"Who is that?" Jo asked at the same time I said, "We have company."

Marlee parked in the circular driveway, and we wasted no time climbing out to see who our visitor was. He turned to face us as we approached the front-porch steps, and I was surprised to see it was Newton Yates.

"We meet again," I said. It was the third time I'd seen the guy in less than a week.

"Oh, Hazel, hello. Good evening, ladies." Newton smiled down at us. He had that look I'd come to recognize as someone who was on the verge of asking a big favor.

"There's going to be an emergency election in two weeks," Newton said. "I'm out canvassing for the vacant spot on the city council."

"You're canvassing already?" Jo asked. "I'm with the newspaper, and the news of an emergency election hasn't even reached me, yet."

"It was just decided tonight," Newton clarified.

"Ah, then Doug got the scoop. He was assigned to cover the meeting tonight."

"I didn't waste any time hitting the campaign trail." Newton's smile grew wider, and Marlee and I exchanged a glance. We knew from our conversation with Newton at the park that he was about to launch into his political spiel. "I really hope I can count on you ladies to vote for me. Rumor has it—"

Newton cut off as he turned his attention to something behind us. His face paled, and he took a step back.

We all turned, expecting to see something scary or awful.

Instead, it was just Wyatt Hightower.

That was scary and awful in its own right, I supposed.

"Newton," Wyatt said, sounding tired and annoyed, "I told you, it's not even official yet. Why are you here?"

CHAPTER NINETEEN

I COULD SEE THE sheen of sweat on Newton's forehead. He pulled out a white handkerchief and dabbed at his face. "I know you said I should wait, but if I'm going to honor Fortie, then I have to make sure I win his seat."

"What's not official, Wyatt?" I asked.

"The city hasn't formally opened to candidates for the vacant city council spot," Wyatt explained. I noticed he was wearing plaid flannel pants and what looked like wool house slippers underneath his long blue coat. He had been ready for bed, even though it wasn't late, and dealing with an overeager citizen had not been in his plans. "Newton knows he's not supposed to canvass until it's official, because it was explained at the meeting tonight. I reminded him about it just ten minutes ago, when he came to my front door."

Newton was still making stabbing motions with his handkerchief, looking like a trapped animal up on my front porch.

Oh, no, he's going to get so nervous that he starts to change.

"Stanley Youngblood had to retire from city council for health reasons a few years back," Jo said. She pulled a small notebook and pen out of her purse, and I had to smile at the sight. Jo sensed there might be a good story for the newspaper, and she was going to get everything on record. "The process to fill his seat took months, and while there was a special election then, too, it didn't come about this quickly after Stanley announced he was leaving."

"The mayor believes swift action is best if we're going to protect Foxfire Haven." Newton looked slightly more confident. He wasn't wiping his brow anymore, at any rate.

"Protect Foxfire Haven from what?" Valerian asked.

"We need a fully functional city council in order to make the best possible decisions for this town," Newton hedged. "It's important to protect our town from bad apples."

I would have been willing to bet Newton was referring to non-magical people. Or, as many citizens of Foxfire Haven called them, *outside people*. I had always disliked the term and the way it implied that people in the mundane world were somehow less than those of us in our little magical town. Less special. Less trustworthy. Less everything.

Since I had lived in the non-magical world for most of my adult life, I had pretty strong feelings about it. People here would look at my own daughter and see her as an unworthy outsider.

I could feel my anger flaring up, and I wanted to dive into a lecture for Newton's benefit. As I was trying to put together what I would say, I suddenly got the mental image of my magic building up to an unsafe level while Newton got more and more uncomfortable. He would be halfway into his transformation into a big, fat bullfrog as my magic exploded out of me, knocking him backward and showering his green reptilian skin in pink sparkles.

The mental image was so ridiculous I began to laugh. I put a hand over my mouth, but it didn't help. Everyone stared at me, and while my coven seemed amused, Newton and Wyatt looked wary. Once I finally got myself under control, I looked at Newton. "I'm laughing, but what you're implying isn't funny at all. You should have stuck to your original platform, Newton. The idea that you wanted to honor your best friend's memory by taking his place on the city council sounded a lot nicer."

"But I am doing it for Fortie!" Newton insisted.

"Go home, Newton," Wyatt said. He sounded utterly exhausted. "And, please, don't stop at anyone else's house along the way."

"But—"

"Do I need to arrest you for harassing these ladies?"

Newton's shoulders slumped. "No. I'll go."

"Can I call you tomorrow to ask some follow-up questions?" Jo asked. Her pen was flying across the page of her notebook.

That seemed to lift Newton's spirits. "Of course. I'll be available all day."

Newton smiled at each of us as he descended the porch steps and moved past our group. "Good night, and don't forget to vote," he said. We watched him walk toward the street, and I spotted a car parked on the curb not far away, which must have been his.

"Chief Constable Hightower, is canvassing before becoming a formal candidate even legal?" Jo asked.

"I haven't the slightest idea. I just found out about all this nonsense when he showed up at my door tonight. I was going to go to bed early."

"You've had a long few days," Marlee said. "Thanks for coming to our rescue, but you should head on home, yourself."

"I will." Wyatt looked at me. "The mayor is trying to get him elected awfully quickly."

I had been right to suspect Euphoria. I could see it in Wyatt's face, the mix of concession and reluctance. Euphoria might have had an alibi for the timeframe of Fortie's murder, but she could have hired someone to kill for her. And, I knew, Wyatt was going to take a much harder look at the mayor.

Gemma's predictions about our futures had been driven out of our heads by the strange encounter with Newton. After he'd left, we'd gone inside to make dinner and eat, and all we could talk about was his eagerness to start his campaign and Euphoria's equal enthusiasm to get him elected.

It was all very suspicious.

When I woke up on Thursday morning, I found all three of my roommates in the kitchen. Jo was toasting bagels while Marlee and Valerian looked through that day's edition of the newspaper.

"Anything exciting?" I asked as I poured myself a cup of coffee.

"No. The news about the emergency election didn't make it into today's edition," Jo said. "But it will for sure be in tomorrow's paper, and I plan to have a story alongside it. It will be a deep dive into Newton and his plans."

I raised an eyebrow. "And I'm guessing the story will not be an endorsement."

"Certainly not. But it won't be mean, either. I'm a fair journalist." Jo grabbed a bagel out of the toaster. "I'm heading to work. Keep me posted if any other politicians show up on our doorstep."

We all wished Jo a good day as she breezed out of the kitchen.

"You're up early, Val," I noted.

"I woke up before my alarm clock, and I thought I'd lay in bed and read for a bit." Valerian sounded annoyed.

"But?" I prompted.

Before Valerian could answer, Marlee said, "I am so jealous. Holman showed up and had a whole conversation with her!"

"You wouldn't be jealous if you'd ever met the ghost. He had a lot to say about why my hair is such a mess in the morning, and how I should be putting it in rollers before I go to bed at night." Valerian's hair was loose that morning, and it looked perfectly fine to me. "Holman also had some choice words about my pajamas."

"I'll scold him the next time I see him," I promised. "He'll pop up as soon as I put on something ugly."

"I'm going to buy the tackiest outfit I can find and parade around the house in it until he shows up to comment," Marlee declared. She had yet to meet Holman, and despite our warnings that it was better that way, she was eager to see our spectral roommate for herself.

After we ate breakfast, Marlee left for a meeting with a new florist she was hoping could create the arrangements for the last-minute, lavish wedding she was planning.

Valerian said she was going to take her book into the living room. "I'll be sure to touch-up my lipstick before I go, so Holman won't come tell me I don't have enough color," she intoned.

That left me to tackle some business work that morning. I had just settled behind Uncle Grant's hulking desk in the office, when my cell phone rang. The man on the other end introduced himself as the manager of an office building downtown, and he asked If I'd come load up what remained in Fortie's office.

"Won't his family want to do that?" I asked.

"They've requested having a service handle it," the man explained. "Some items have been earmarked for delivery to the family, and the rest is going to a second-hand store."

The local thrift stores were getting a big boost in inventory lately.

The hastiness of clearing out Fortie's office felt disrespectful, somehow. It hadn't even been a week since his murder, but his professional life was already being cleared away. It felt even more bizarre than the speed at which Fortie's spot on the city council was being filled.

Still, if the family had requested it, then who was I to turn down the work? I agreed to be at the office building by one o'clock that day, got the address, and ended the call, feeling grateful for the income. I also sensed the irony of the situation. Even though I had never met Fortie when he was alive, our paths continued to cross now that he was dead.

The office building was one street behind city hall, making it a convenient spot for Fortie to have had his office. The lush carpeting and elegant light fixtures in the lobby hinted that Fortie had been quite successful in his career. I couldn't imagine the offices there were cheap to rent.

Despite the posh lobby, though, Fortie's office felt like a time capsule. There were dark rugs covering the wooden floorboards, and the desk that sat between two tall windows rivaled the one Uncle Grant had used at the funeral home. It didn't take much looking around to realize Fortie had been an investment broker. There were boxes of files already packed and ready to go, plus a pile of business cards and notepads in the center of the desk.

"We're just finishing up," said a woman who was hastily transferring manila file folders from a filing cabinet into a brown cardboard box.

"And I'll help you get everything loaded up," said a voice coming from underneath the desk. A moment later, a man's head emerged, followed slowly by the rest of him as he grunted and pulled himself up to a standing position. "Okay, the phone and computer are unplugged."

The man I had spoken to on the phone arrived just a moment later, wheeling a cart so we could carry everything down to the hearse.

After half an hour, the hearse was absolutely crammed full of stuff. It was the biggest delivery job I'd had yet.

Just as I was swinging the rear door of the hearse shut, a man in a tailored gray suit walked up to me. He looked like he was about my age, and he had an expression of polite interest on his face. "Did someone die?"

"I run a delivery service," I explained. "The hearse is great for hauling things around."

The man looked like he wasn't sure whether to laugh or be horrified. He settled for returning to his polite expression as he said, "Well, I'm relieved to hear Fortie Fortenbacher hasn't bitten the dust. He's the one I'm here to see."

I stared at the man, unsure how to break the news to him.

Thankfully, the woman who had been packing files came to my rescue. "I'm sorry to tell you that Fortie was murdered last Friday. Haven't you seen the news?"

The man's face paled. "No. I live in Stanton. Murdered? How? Who?"

"My condolences," I said. "Were you a friend of Fortie's?"

"He was a client. We had a meeting today to discuss my company's proposal." The man tilted the folder he had in his hand, and I caught a red logo that included two ornate *P*s entwined inside a circle.

The woman told him to come inside so she could fill him in. Once the two of them were gone, I was by myself, so I headed out. My first stop would be at the home of Fortie's sister, who was taking all of the business and personal things that had come out of the office. After that, the more generic pieces were heading to the thrift store just outside of downtown Foxfire Haven.

When I finally reached the thrift store, an employee and I unloaded the mini fridge that had been in Fortie's office. We had laid it on its back for the trip to the store, and it was easy to pull out of the hearse, thanks to the built-in rollers that had been installed for getting caskets in and out.

The employee pulled the door of the fridge open. "Why does no one ever check these before donating them?" He pulled out a soggy-looking sandwich and a can of soda.

Inside the freezer was a bag of peas.

"I'll take those off your hands," I offered. I was thinking back to what Gemma had said about her death prediction for Newton. She had speculated that Newton had either altered his fate or that the peas had been tainted with Fortie's energy.

It was time to find out for certain.

CHAPTER TWENTY

THE PEAS WERE STILL frozen, since the mini fridge had been unplugged only an hour before. I figured I didn't have a lot of time before they began to thaw, though, so once I had gotten the hearse emptied out at the thrift store, I made a beeline for Gemma's house.

She would be surprised to see me again so soon, unless she had divined her own future in the peas and saw me coming.

Luck was with me when I turned onto Gemma's street, because there was an empty space right in front of her house that was big enough for the hearse.

Unfortunately, luck was not with me when I got to the front door and saw a handwritten sign taped to it. Gemma had written that she was out of peas and had gone to the store to restock.

There was no telling how long that might take, so I reluctantly headed home and stashed the peas in the freezer. I would just have to wait to find out if any of Fortie's presence was sticking to the frozen vegetables.

Perkins flew into the kitchen to see what I was up to, and as I poured myself a glass of water, he hooted in a way I'd come to recognize as him asking me how things were going. The sound rose in pitch at the end, like he was asking a question.

"I'm okay. Just feeling thoughtful," I said. I gestured around the kitchen. "Uncle Grant died, and my parents came out here to pack up his personal items. Then, when Dad died, my brother and I went to Florida to help Mom. But Fortie gets murdered, and his stuff is being loaded up by strangers and sent to charity before he's been dead a week. Doesn't that seem odd to you?"

In answer, Perkins tilted his head until it was completely sideways.

"Exactly. People in town say Fortie wasn't always the most popular guy because of the power trip he was on as a city councilman, but I'm starting to think his family didn't care that much for him, either. How sad."

Perkins hopped over to the basket containing the items I'd been using for my kindness spell. I'd left the basket on the windowsill, and the candle was at the top of the pile. He tapped his beak against the candle, then looked at me with his bright-yellow eyes.

"You're right. If Fortie had practiced kindness, people would be treating his memory with more kindness now. It's a good lesson."

Satisfied that he'd gotten his point across, Perkins fluttered to his nest, fluffed up the strips of flannel with his feet, then curled into a ball.

I waited as patiently as I could, but after an hour of thinking about doing housework and not actually getting started, I gave up and left the house with Fortie's peas in one hand. I had gotten rid of my regular car to save money, which meant I had to get to Gemma's either in the hearse or on my bicycle. It was too far to walk.

The slow but steady rain outside convinced me to drive. The gray clouds had lowered since I'd made the delivery run of Fortie's office contents, and it looked like the kind of rain that would be settling in for a while.

My parking luck had run out by the time I got to Gemma's. I had to park three streets away, since none of the closer spots on the curb were long enough for the hearse. There were a couple places I probably could have squeezed into, but my parallel parking skills in that thing were not very good. Not yet, at least.

Only one person was standing in front of Gemma's house, and the note on the door had disappeared. That meant my wait wouldn't be too long, and soon, Gemma was ushering me into the dining room.

"I can't say I'm surprised to see you again so soon," Gemma said as I settled into an empty chair. "I saw your relationship to Fortie's murder during your coven's reading, but you want to know more about your life. You're a curious woman."

"Who isn't curious about their future?" I asked, handing over the bag of peas. I didn't mention they had come from Fortie's office, since I wanted to see if Gemma naturally picked up on any kind of association with him.

"You'd be surprised," Gemma said as she snipped off the top of the bag with a pair of scissors. "There are a lot of people who are too scared to know what's going to happen to them."

Gemma repeated the same process she had the day before, slowly pouring the entire bag of peas in a circle around the cluster of candles. Just seconds after they had stopped rolling around and settled into place, Gemma moaned loudly.

"Are you okay?" I asked, half-rising from my chair. When Gemma clutched at her chest, I worried she was having some kind of medical emergency.

"Death! Death!" Gemma wailed.

I stood fully and moved closer to Gemma, nearly slipping when I stepped on a clump of peas. I waved my arms wildly to steady myself. Once I knew I wasn't going to topple over, I said, "I'll call for an ambulance!"

Gemma's look of agony turned into one of annoyance. "Not for me," she scolded. "For you. I see death for you!"

Strangely, despite Gemma predicting my death, I felt a wave of relief. I was more comfortable with the idea of my future demise than her dropping dead right there in the middle of the dining room.

Plus, I wasn't sure Gemma was seeing my death, at all. Fortie's peas might have caused another wrong prediction.

"Where?" I asked.

"The peas aren't that detailed. I just see the sign for your death, not where it's going to happen."

I shook my head. "I meant, where is the death omen?" I looked down at the floor, but all I saw was a lot of green peas glowing in the candlelight.

"There." Gemma pointed to a cluster of peas near a chair leg. "You see how they form a skull shape?"

I saw the peas in question, but to my untrained eyes, they formed the shape of a wonky star. At least, they did if I squinted and tilted my head.

Gemma let out a frustrated sigh. "Come to where I'm standing."

I did as instructed, and as soon as I looked at the peas from Gemma's vantage point, I could easily make out the skull. "Wow. It's so clear from this angle."

"Indeed. And, since I'm the reader, it's this angle that matters."

I stepped closer to the shape and bent down to brush my fingers against it. *How strange that people are willing to turn their lives upside down, all because of what a few peas look like to an old woman.*

The peas under my fingers shifted. When they did, the rest of the peas in the death omen shifted with them, but the cluster maintained its shape. I pushed again, harder this time. The whole group of peas moved as one.

I pinched one of the peas between my thumb and forefinger, then lifted. The entire clump of peas came off the ground.

"Gemma," I said, turning to her with the skull dangling from my fingers. "Someone glued these peas together to look like a death omen."

CHAPTER TWENTY-ONE

GEMMA WAS SO STILL for so long I again considered calling for an ambulance. She stared at the peas I was holding, a look of absolute shock on her face. Finally, she made a choking sound, then moaned. "I don't understand."

"I found this bag of peas in Fortie's office," I confessed. "They were in his mini fridge. You'd mentioned Newton's death omen might have been meant for Fortie, because he also showed up here with a bag of Fortie's peas. I wanted to see if it happened again."

"And it did, but not because Fortie's energy was attached to the bag." Gemma's eyes slid to the plastic bag, which she'd discarded on one of the empty chairs.

"Let's see if we can figure out how it was done." I reached out to grab the bag, then realized it might be evidence in Fortie's murder. Someone had been manipulating Fortie's peas so he would think he was going to die. The question was, had that same person also killed him?

My fingerprints would be all over the bag. Fortie and Gemma had touched it, too. But, maybe, the constables could find another set of fingerprints that would help them get answers.

So, instead of picking up the bag, I leaned down close to it. "Gemma, can you please turn on the lights?" When she complied, I could see the resealable top on the bag. Gemma had cut the bag open, but it could have simply been opened like a zip-top bag.

I turned a slow circle until my eyes landed on the lopped-off top of the bag. The long, plastic strip was in two pieces, rather than sealed together at the top. I hadn't noticed when I'd grabbed the peas that the bag had been opened previously. Gemma hadn't spotted it, either, thanks in part to the low lighting inside the room.

I was willing to bet Fortie hadn't noticed someone was opening his bags of peas, either. Otherwise, he would have realized his death predictions were all staged.

Carefully, I put the cluster of peas back down where I'd found them. "You told us some of your chickens hadn't been doing well recently. I'm sure whatever glue was used to make these shapes wasn't good for them."

Gemma blew out a breath and sat down hard in the nearest chair. "And, since Fortie died, there haven't been any glued peas coming here, which is why the chickens are doing better. Fortie was coming to me almost daily in the last few weeks of his life. My poor chickens! They were almost murdered, too."

"I'm going to call the constables." I was already picking up my purse so I could fish my phone out of it. "They're going to want to collect all of this as evidence."

"But I have clients outside, waiting for their readings! I don't want to lose that money!" Suddenly, Gemma's face brightened. "Never mind. I can use this to my advantage. When word gets out that the constables had to come here again as part of their investigation, even more people will want to use my services."

Instead of calling the general number for the Foxfire Haven Constables, I called Wyatt directly. He had once given me his business card, and I was happy I'd put it in my purse.

I briefly told Wyatt what had happened, promising that Gemma and I would fill him in on the details once he arrived. I ended the call in time to hear Gemma talking to herself. "I'll head to the tavern this evening and let it drop that the constables had to come here to collect evidence. Oh, I'll have a crowd tomorrow!" She cackled and clapped her hands together.

We didn't have long to wait for Wyatt and several other constables to arrive. Soon, they were inside the dining room, asking questions and taking photos. Wyatt assigned a constable named Donna to take my statement, and I explained how I'd been hired to take away everything from Fortie's office. The entire time I spoke, Wyatt kept looking over at me. I got the sense he wanted to say something, but for some reason, he was holding back.

While I had been telling my side of the story, Gemma had been doing the same for another constable. She had a lot more to tell, since she'd been reading various death omens in Fortie's peas for months. Someone had been keeping up the charade for a long time.

I listened in on Gemma's story for a few minutes before I felt a gentle hand on my elbow, steering me away from the others. It was Wyatt, and once we were a few feet away, he said quietly, "The others can wrap up here. You're coming with me."

I'm being arrested, I thought. *Wyatt Hightower is going to put me in handcuffs and throw me in jail because he thinks I killed Fortie.*

I blinked a few times as I tried to steady my thoughts. That was a ridiculous idea. I hadn't even known Fortie, and I wasn't a suspect in this case. Whatever Wyatt wanted, it wasn't to arrest me.

Wyatt didn't say another word as he led me out to his patrol car. The sedan was a bit old but clean and well-kept. I felt very official sitting in the passenger seat, and I was grateful not to be in the back, like I'd initially pictured in my head.

"Where are we going?" I asked as Wyatt pulled away from the curb.

"I need coffee."

When it was clear Wyatt wasn't going to give me any more details, I sat back and did my best to ignore him. It was still raining, and I relaxed as we rolled past the dripping fir trees.

Wyatt drove us downtown, then parked in front of the Salt Circle. He was still silent as he held the door of the cafe open for me. It wasn't until we were seated and he'd ordered a pot of coffee with two cups that he said, "Why were you at Gemma's again?"

"I told you. There was a bag of peas in the freezer of Fortie's mini fridge, and I wanted to test Gemma's theory that they were holding on to some of his energy."

Wyatt gazed at me, stone-faced.

"I was curious, okay?" I knew I sounded like a petulant teenager.

Our server swept up and quickly placed a stainless steel pot of coffee plus two ceramic mugs on the table.

I jumped at the chance to break eye contact with Wyatt and busied myself with pouring our coffee. "What do you take?"

"Just one spoonful of sugar."

I doled out the sugar and began stirring it into Wyatt's coffee. "Gemma's theory was wrong, of course," I continued. "The death omen she saw for Newton was just glued-together peas that had been meant for Fortie."

"You weren't at Gemma's solely out of curiosity."

I slid Wyatt's cup toward him, then met his gaze again. I did, however, lift my own mug so it half-hid my face. Wyatt had a way of looking at me that made me feel like he was seeing into my mind. It was uncomfortable.

"You're still trying to solve this murder." Wyatt curled two fingers through the handle of his mug. With his other hand, he smoothed back his silver hair. "What I want to know is why. What are you trying to prove?"

"I'm not trying to solve the murder. I called you when I realized the peas were connected to the murder, didn't I? I didn't try to figure it out myself."

"The only reason you were with the fortune-teller in the first place is because you want to know who killed Fortie."

There was a sinking feeling in my stomach. He was right.

My shoulders slumped as I stared down into my steaming mug. "Everywhere I go, someone says something about the murder. It's as if Fortie keeps popping up in my life, like when I got the call to take away the things in his office. I keep saying I'm not trying to solve this murder, and that's true. I want to help, if I can, though I'm certainly not going after suspects myself. But..."

I paused, searching for the right words. Finally, I put down my coffee and spread my hands. "It's like the murder is trying to get itself solved, and it keeps dropping clues into my lap." I sighed and let my hands fall, palms down, onto the table. "I'm sure that sounds stupid."

"What kind of a witch are you?"

I was caught off guard by the sudden turn in the conversation, and it took me a moment to realize what Wyatt was asking. Finally, with a scoff, I said, "A bad one, as you well know."

"You know what I mean. What is your specialty? Where is your magic the strongest?"

"Petunia Cornwell called me a mom witch. I've always been the prepared one, able to know just what to pack for a trip or coming up with detailed plans for scenarios that are unlikely but wind up happening, anyway."

"Intuitive."

When I nodded, Wyatt smiled softly. "Your magic is in a deep knowing. Not in foresight, like Gemma or other divination experts, but in intuitive anticipation. I assume you often find yourself in the right place at the right time."

"Not exactly the kind of magic that lands you a good job." And, I reminded myself, it was one of the reasons I'd been so eager to leave Foxfire Haven after graduation. My witchcraft was never going to be strong enough to get me a good magical job, but my organizational skills had served me well in the mundane world.

"Are you kidding?" Wyatt leaned forward, his expression excited. "It's an incredibly valuable kind of magic. I said once before that you'd be a good detective, and this is partly why. Your talent is in solving problems, even if they haven't happened yet. You're pulling on so many threads connected to Fortie's murder, because you see possibilities the rest of us can't. You just haven't found the one that weaves them all together yet."

As Wyatt had been talking, I'd felt my hands start to shake with excitement. I'd picked up my coffee mug again, but I had to put it down because the hot liquid was in danger of sloshing over the side. Wyatt was framing my magic in a way no one ever had before. Not even my parents had viewed my abilities through that kind of a lens. Suddenly, I was looking at my magic in a whole new light.

Maybe I'm not as bad of a witch as I thought.

I was flattered, but I was also feeling a bit flustered. I wasn't used to getting compliments like the one Wyatt had just paid me, and the fact that it was coming from him, when he disliked me so much, put me even further outside my comfort zone.

Slowly, I lifted my mug. My hands had stopped shaking, so I took a few sips of my coffee while I tried to process everything Wyatt had just said. I was also trying to think of the appropriate response when he continued talking. "You need to be careful, though, before you get yourself in trouble."

"I've been practicing," I assured him. "I'm learning to control my magic, so I don't have any more...incidents."

"I'm not talking about that. I mean, you need to watch your step. I don't want Fortie's killer coming after you when they realize you're getting close to the truth."

I looked at the people sitting in the booths near ours, suddenly wondering if someone among them had killed

Fortie. "Do you think I'm in danger?" I asked, my voice barely above a whisper.

"I hope not, but please be careful." Wyatt looked genuinely concerned for my safety, and there was a kindness in his eyes. "Stick close to your coven until we solve this case."

"I will. And I'll call you if I stumble across any more leads."

Wyatt and I barely spoke as we both drank our coffee. He pulled a small notebook out of his pocket and wrote some things down, and I figured he was deep in thought about the manipulated peas. I had my own thoughts to deal with, so the silence didn't feel awkward in the slightest.

I was finishing my cup of coffee when Wyatt stirred himself from his thoughts. "I'll drive you back to Gemma's house."

"No need. I'm going to go across the street to catch up with Val, so I'll get the hearse later."

Wyatt pointed a finger at me. "I meant what I said. Be careful."

I had to promise to be alert for danger three more times before Wyatt and I parted in front of the cafe.

Soon, though, I was settled on a barstool at the tavern, a bowl of chili steaming in front of me. Barry was at his usual spot, and he'd turned and given me a smile when I came in before returning to brooding over his whiskey.

When there was movement to my right, I looked to see Newton clambering onto the vacant stool next to me. He tugged at the collar of his white button-down shirt. "I heard about the doctored peas," he said to me.

"Already?" Gemma hadn't wasted any time spreading the word.

"I just can't believe it. She was gluing Fortie's peas to make it look like he was going to die!"

"No. Gemma didn't know about the deception, either. She's innocent in this."

"I'm not talking about Gemma. I mean the witch Fortie was getting the peas from: Melba Hawthorn!"

CHAPTER TWENTY-TWO

"WHY WOULD MELBA GLUE Fortie's peas into the shapes of death omens?" It made zero sense to me. "And why was Fortie getting his peas from Melba in the first place?"

Newton looked equally confused as he answered, "Fortie was buying peas from Melba because she told him they were charmed to give a more accurate reading. Fortie trusted Melba with his life. I can't figure out why she would do something so awful to him."

"You have to tell the constables," I said.

Newton shook his head, then tugged again at the collar of his shirt. He was breathing heavier. "No. I can't do that! They'll charge Melba with fraudulent magic. She could lose her business license."

Valerian had been standing nearby, and she leaned over the bar to give Newton a stern look. "You should be more worried they'll charge her with murder."

"What?" Newton's chest heaved, and he looked from Valerian to me. "Why would anyone think she killed Fortie?"

"I agree it seems unlikely," I said. I'd initially suspected Melba of murdering Fortie to boost her business, but as time had gone on, I'd realized how much of a reach that was. "If Fortie was paying her regularly, why kill him?"

Valerian nodded. "Good point. Melba would have kept her scam going, continuing to manipulate the peas so Fortie would continue paying her gobs of money to help ward off his fate." Valerian gave Newton a reassuring smile. "So, I suppose losing her business license really is all she needs to be worried about."

"I don't want to do that to her," Newton said. "She's always been so nice to me."

"If she was lying to Fortie, then who else has she done something like this to?" I pressed my index finger against my chest. "Newton, if you don't tell the constables, I will."

"Or, maybe..." Valerian began.

"You have a new theory?" I asked. Beside me, Newton was continuing to look distressed. If his eyes started bulging, or if I detected a hint of green in his skin, I was going to haul him outside and do a calming spell on him.

Which, of course, had the potential to backfire horribly on me.

"We've been discounting Melba as a suspect because we're looking at it from a financial angle," Valerian explained. "Why would she kill her cash cow? But, maybe, she's been plotting this since the first time she glued Fortie's peas together. Maybe she wanted to torment him before killing him."

I frowned. "You think this was about revenge?"

"Maybe. Like we told you when Fortie died, there aren't a ton of folks in Foxfire Haven who will be devastated by the loss. Maybe he clashed with Melba, like he did with so many other business owners in town."

"What do you mean?" Newton cried. "Fortie was a good man! We're all devastated by the loss."

"He liked to wield his city council position like a weapon," Valerian said. She kept her tone gentle, probably because she was reading the same signs I was. Newton was on the verge of shifting. "Unfortunately, your best friend ruffled a lot of feathers in the business community."

"I thought," Newton began. He grabbed a napkin and wiped it across his forehead. "That is, Fortie always made himself sound like a hero. He was working hard for our businesses."

Newton's chest began to spasm, as if he had the hiccups. His breath started to come in shallow gasps, and on one exhale, I heard a distinct "*ribbit.*"

"Come on," I said, grabbing Newton by the forearm. "Let's go outside. Deep breaths, Newton. Focus."

"I'll catch up!" Valerian called.

Newton walked like someone who was drunk as I propelled him out the back door of the tavern. Once we were in the narrow alley out back, I turned to Newton and took both of his hands in mine. "Look at me, Newton."

He did, and I didn't like it one bit. Newton's eyes were already starting to shift, making them bulge as he stared at me with a panicked expression.

"Loop me in!" Valerian appeared next to me, and I dropped one of Newton's hands to take hers. She, in turn, grabbed Newton's fingers in a tight grip. "Go ahead, Haze."

I opened my mouth to recite the calming spell I frequently used on myself, then hesitated. "Maybe you should do it, Val. You're a better witch than I am."

"Nonsense. You can do this, but I'm right here to help if you need me."

I braced myself, then focused again on Newton. His nose looked like it was beginning to shrink back into his face, and his lips were growing wider. "Focus on me, Newton. You have magic from both Val and me working for you." I began to recite the words of the calming spell, realizing as I did so that I needed it just as much as Newton did.

It was a tense few minutes as I repeated the spell over and over again, but slowly, Newton's breathing began to slow down. His nose stopped shrinking and returned to its normal size and shape. Finally, Newton shut his eyes tight as he drew in a slow breath. When he opened them again, they had returned to normal.

"I'm okay," Newton assured me. He looked tired and embarrassed.

"Come on," Valerian told him. "I've got an elixir that will fix you right up. Made it myself." She led Newton back inside while calling over her shoulder, "Well done, Hazel! I told you so!"

I grinned as Valerian and Newton disappeared through the door. I stayed outside a few minutes longer, and I even said my incantation to shed any excess magic I'd built up. I was happy to see only a bit of my pink magic puff out, which meant I was getting better at controlling it.

Newton was already halfway through a blue drink when I returned to my stool at the bar. He stopped slurping it down long enough to thank me, and as he did, I could smell chamomile and knew the elixir Valerian had given him was to continue keeping him calm.

"Thanks for adding your magic, Val," I said as she came over to me with a red drink in her hands.

"Happy to help." She plunked the tall, skinny glass down in front of me. "Have this, on the house. It's called a Victor's Vial. When you've achieved something significant, you drink this to extend the feeling of accomplishment."

I lifted the glass and raised it in a little salute. "Here's to being in the right place at the right time." I thought of what Wyatt had just been telling me over our coffee at The Salt Circle. The murder seemed to be throwing itself in my way so I could help solve it. Newton showing up and telling me that Melba had been the one doctoring the peas was just another sign of that.

Is this my magic? I wondered. *Am I drawing the clues to myself?*

That was a silly idea. To the best of my knowledge, there was no such thing as a clue witch. Or a detective witch. Though, I had to admit, I did like the sound of that. Hazel Underwood, Foxfire Haven's finest detective witch. It had a nice ring to it.

Whatever kind of witch I was, figuring it out wasn't the most important thing at the moment. "Newton," I said, putting a hand on his arm, "I'm sorry to harp on this, but the constables need to know about Melba being the one behind the peas."

Newton put down his empty glass. "Yes, I know. And thanks to you and the best bartender in Foxfire Haven, I'm ready to go tell them."

I gave Newton some words of encouragement as he slid off his barstool and headed toward the door. I watched him go, then turned back to the bar with a sigh.

"He's a shifter?" Barry asked. He was staring in the direction Newton had gone.

"Bullfrog."

"How unfortunate." Barry turned back to his drink, and I had to stifle a laugh. He never said much from his perch at the bar, but he always made it count.

My chili was cold by the time I started to eat it, and Valerian took the bowl away to get me a fresh one. After I had another bowl of steaming chili in front of me, I started eating before any more magical mayhem could interrupt me. I had worked up an appetite between being under Wyatt's scrutiny and helping Newton calm down.

When both my Victor's Vial and my chili were gone, I paid and was on the verge of leaving when I realized the hearse was still at Gemma's. I decided I could walk home. Despite Wyatt's warnings, I had a hard time believing that walking home in broad daylight would put me in any kind of danger.

Before I could do that, though, Julian came into the bar. I already had one foot on the ground when I spotted him, and I quickly resettled myself on the stool. Maybe, I thought, Julian would drop some useful information, too.

Valerian must have known what I was doing, because she gestured to the empty stool beside me. "Why don't you take this one, Councilman?"

Julian didn't argue with that, and after ordering a vodka tonic from Valerian, he added, "I just saw Newtie on his way out. Did he tell you the news?"

Once again, I had to concentrate on not laughing. Newtie and Fortie? No wonder they had been best friends.

Valerian was better at keeping a poker face than I was. "You mean the news about Melba and her death peas?"

"I never thought she'd do something like that."

"I did," Valerian quipped. She moved off to make Julian's drink.

"It's just shocking, isn't it?" I asked, hoping Julian would keep talking.

"One shock after another this week." He pulled his phone out of his pocket, since it was buzzing, and he held it to his ear. When he spoke, his voice was back to its usual booming, confident tone. "Julian Ashcroft here."

When Julian proceeded to have a very loud conversation with whomever was on the other end of the call, I gave up and left.

I was only half a block from the tavern when I heard a honk, and Marlee's car pulled to a stop next to me. The passenger-side window lowered, and Marlee leaned across the seat to get a look at me. "Need a ride?"

I quickly said yes, and soon, I was filling Marlee in on the news as she drove.

"This will go down in history as the Foxfire Haven pea scandal," Marlee said when I had finished. "I know I shouldn't be making fun of such a serious situation, but it really does sound ridiculous."

"No argument there."

"By the way, I have my own news to share." Marlee shot me a wicked look. "But I'm going to wait until we're home, because I want to be looking right at you when I say it, so I can enjoy your reaction."

Instead of taking me home, though, Marlee took me to my car. As I thanked her for the ride and climbed into the hearse, I noticed there were five people patiently lined up outside Gemma's house. Apparently, the constables had finished collecting the evidence, and she had things up and running again.

I followed Marlee on the drive home, and as soon as we were both inside the funeral home and had our coats off, I said, "Okay, spill your news."

Marlee insisted we sit down at the kitchen table first so she could properly enjoy my reaction.

"While you were having your own adventures today," she said, "I was with Melba Hawthorn."

I gasped. "You got in for a reading with her?"

"No. I barged into her office when she was between clients, claiming I was there because I wanted to team up. I told her the birthday ritual recommendation was much appreciated, and that I hoped we might have more opportunities to combine our services." Marlee was beaming, clearly proud of herself.

"What in the world inspired you to do that?"

"I wanted to know how Melba had wound up with my business card in the first place. I figured the pretense of teaming up was a good way to have a chat with her."

"And? Who gave your card to her?"

"You're not going to believe this. I was recommended to Melba by your least-favorite person in Foxfire Haven!"

I gaped at Marlee. "It was Wyatt who told her about your business?"

Marlee laughed, her body shaking with delight. "No! Not Wyatt. Mayor Lachlan, of course."

CHAPTER TWENTY-THREE

I STARTED LAUGHING ALONG with Marlee. "Oh, yeah. Euphoria. How could I forget her?"

"Besides, you just had a coffee date with Chief Constable Hightower." Marlee grinned wickedly. "He can't be your least-favorite person in town."

"It was not a date." I was going to argue the point some more, but instead, I said, "If Euphoria gave Melba your card, I wonder if it has any relevance to Fortie's murder. Jo said Euphoria and Fortie used to clash all the time."

"And, now, we know Euphoria is friendly with the witch who made Fortie think he was going to die."

"And Melba must have had some motivation for doing that. Which means..." I trailed off. What did it mean?

Marlee nodded. "That's as far as I've gotten, too. When I was talking to Melba, her emotions were telling me loud and clear that she's hiding a secret. But whether that secret was about the peas, the murder, or something wholly unrelated, I don't know."

"It's a shame you can take on others' emotions but can't tell exactly why someone is feeling what they feel."

"I'm just happy to have more detail about how my card wound up in Fortie's pocket."

"It's entirely possible Euphoria hired Melba to doctor the peas. Maybe she was trying to send Fortie a warning," I mused. "Jo could do some digging and tell us if the two of them were fighting about a city issue back when Fortie first began to get the signs."

"We know Jo is already looking for connections in past newspaper coverage."

"Newton was going to tell the constables that Melba was behind the death omens," I said. "We'll let the constables figure out the rest. I'm staying out of it."

"Sure you are." Stella and Perkins both zoomed through the open window at that moment. As Perkins landed on the table directly in front of me, Stella fluttered down onto Marlee's shoulder.

Marlee looked at the toucan. "Do you believe Hazel is staying out of it?"

Stella waggled her long beak back and forth, and Marlee giggled. "I agree. Here's what I can't figure out, though."

It took me a moment to realize Marlee was talking to me again rather than to her familiar.

"Euphoria hired a wedding planner from Stanton for her big day, rather than coming to me," Marlee continued. "I heard it wasn't a good experience, but that's beside the point. Euphoria must have grabbed some of my cards at one of the city events I was hired to plan, because she's never been a customer of mine."

"She was probably too stuck-up to hire a local company for her wedding," I said with a sniff. "At least she was nice enough to recommend you to someone else, though. I'm sure she felt confident doing that because you have a good reputation."

"A good reputation, and good taste."

I glanced over to see Holman. His ghostly form was shimmering in the doorway between the kitchen and the back hall.

"Do you think you could give Hazel some fashion pointers?" he asked.

Marlee grinned. "Holman! It's so nice to finally meet you! I'm Marlee Yamada."

"Yes, of course you are. I know who's living under my roof." Holman turned his dour look on me. "She's a smart dresser, but perhaps not very bright."

"Holman," I warned.

Marlee very politely ignored the snub from Holman. Instead, she asked, "If you knew I was here, then why are you just now showing up to say hello?"

"Because I don't waste energy materializing just to greet someone." Holman reached up to adjust his suit jacket. "I come along when my advice is needed. You always look very nice, so I haven't had anything to say to you."

"We like getting compliments, you know," Marlee told him. "You could show up to tell us when we're making smart fashion choices."

Holman looked appreciatively at Marlee. "That's not a bad idea. It would help Hazel learn what looks *do* work in her favor. I'll take it under consideration."

Holman disappeared while I was looking down at my jeans and green sweater. What was wrong with my outfit? Had Holman showed up to criticize it, then gotten distracted by Marlee before saying anything?

I decided it was best not to worry about it. Holman's fashion sense was nearly a century out of date, anyway.

There was still a lot of afternoon ahead of me, despite how much had happened already that day. I slowly got tasks done around the house, but the hours dragged past. "Longest Thursday ever," I complained to the portrait of the severe-looking man in the back hallway.

Finally, though, the afternoon gave way to evening. By the time I traded in my possibly unfashionable jeans and sweater for my definitely unfashionable pink-plaid flannel pajamas, I was yawning every thirty seconds.

I had just slid under the covers, when there was a loud knock on my door. "Come in," I called.

Marlee flung open the door and rushed inside, her movements frantic. "Coven emergency! At the tavern!"

"What happened?"

"I don't know." Marlee waved her hands, and I thought I saw faint sparks of her dark-red magic shoot out of her fingertips. "Val called and said we all need to get there immediately. Let's go!"

"Okay. I'll get dressed."

"No time! Come on!"

It was only then I noticed Marlee was wearing her navy-blue silk pajamas underneath her thick black coat. She had added a pair of galoshes to the ensemble, probably because they were close at hand and quick to pull on.

Holman would have some choice words about that look.

I slid into a pair of sandals, silently apologizing to my toes for the cold they were about to endure. As I followed Marlee to her car, I pulled on my coat and zipped it all the way to the top. "Where's Jo?" I asked.

"Val said she's there already."

Marlee broke the speed limit the entire drive into downtown Foxfire Haven. I'd never seen her so wild, and I considered performing the same calming spell I'd used on Newton. Valerian must have been in quite the emotional state when she'd called Marlee, and Marlee had absorbed all that anxious energy.

On the plus side, we made it to the tavern in record time. Marlee parked terribly, her car nowhere close to the curb, but I wasn't about to suggest she try again. We both bolted out of the car and sprinted for the tavern door.

When we walked inside, I knew immediately why Valerian had called it a coven emergency. A woman was standing in the center of the tavern, her black hair hanging in limp strands in front of her face and her long green dress torn at the hem. She had both arms held out to her sides as she looked around wildly.

There were three constables standing just to the left of the front door. "Melba, please," one of them said. She took a tentative step toward the witch, and I realized I was getting my first look at the notorious Melba Hawthorn.

"I said no!" Melba cried in a high-pitched voice. Her right arm stretched toward the constable, and a jet of orange magic shot out of her palm.

The constable ducked, and the magic hit the wall behind her, exploding into a shower of orange sparks. "Assaulting a constable can result in jail time," the constable warned.

Archer, who had been my electrician until I found out he was snooping around my house for the alleged treasure Uncle Grant had been obsessed with, slowly rose from his spot in one of the booths. "Let me have a chat with her."

"Stop trying to help them!" Melba's left arm moved toward Archer, who wisely jumped sideways, narrowly avoiding another stream of orange magic.

Melba swayed and stumbled. She grabbed for the nearest thing to catch her balance, which happened to be a man trying to walk toward the front door. As soon as Melba let go of his jacket sleeve, the man made it to the door in just two strides, a terrified look on his face. Marlee and I stepped apart from each other to give him space to pass.

The man opened the door, and when he did, Stella and Perkins flew inside.

"They followed!" I said.

"Our familiars know when there's trouble. Look." Marlee nodded toward the bar, and I spotted Lonnie and Gordon. Lonnie was perched on a glass bottle that contained some kind of purple potion. Gordon was seated on a barstool next to Jo.

Valerian sidled up to us. "I never even served her! She showed up this drunk. She walked in the door and started yelling about how she's innocent. Now, whenever someone tries to approach her, she throws a curse at them."

"Isn't that against the law?" I asked. I kept my voice low, not wanting to draw Melba's drunken ire.

"Oh, yeah. She's got more than doctored peas to worry about now."

"Why do you need us?" Marlee asked.

"To fight magic with magic." Valerian waved toward Jo, who gracefully slid off her stool and made her way to us, giving Melba as wide of a berth as she could.

Once Jo joined us, Valerian took her hand, then mine. I reached out to put my other hand into Marlee's. It wasn't the first time our coven had joined together to make magic inside the tavern. Then, though, we'd simply been standing up to a mean old man. This time, we were going up against a powerful witch who had lost her self-control.

"We're going to do a binding spell," Valerian told us quietly. "It will bind Melba's magic long enough for the constables to move in and arrest her."

Valerian began to recite words while the rest of us listened closely so we could learn the incantation. Marlee was the first to join in, then Jo and I followed. Once all four of us were speaking the spell, we began to raise our voices, which would help raise our magic, too.

We had begun to repeat the spell for the third time when Melba finally noticed us. She glared at us, her body slowly swaying. "No," she growled.

None of us reacted to her. Instead, we continued with the spell.

With a yell, Melba raised both her hands toward us. The moment her magic burst from her palms, I tightened my grip on Valerian's and Marlee's hands, even as I bent my knees and ducked my head to avoid the curse.

CHapter Twenty-Four

MELBA'S CURSE NEVER EVEN made it to us. The twin beams of magic exploded against an unseen barrier in front of us, orange sparkles falling to the ground to puddle there like melted pumpkins.

Valerian's voice was stronger than ever. She hadn't flinched when Melba had flung her curse at us. Jo, Marlee, and I had all faltered, but we quickly regained our confidence. I was pretty sure that invisible wall had come from us, our bond as a coven creating a protective barrier.

We continued reciting the binding spell, and our four familiars lined up on the floor in front of us. They were lending their energy to our work.

Melba staggered in our direction, then raised her arms again. The magic that shot out of her palms on her second attempt to curse us was paler, and it dissipated into the air before it could hit the protective barrier.

A third attempt was even less powerful, and Melba seemed to realize her magic was going to continue declining. Her arms dropped to her sides, and she hung her head, her long hair sliding over her face.

Tentatively, the constable who had tried to approach Melba previously stepped forward. When Melba didn't react, she quickly closed the distance between them. In just moments, Fortie's trusted magical adviser was in handcuffs.

The constables and Melba all exited the tavern, and once the door had closed behind them, there was silence. Finally, Archer said loudly, "I think we could all use another drink."

There was a buzz as people agreed with that pronouncement, and Valerian quickly moved behind the bar so she could take orders. Jo returned to her barstool with Marlee and me on her heels.

"Sorry, Gordon," I told Jo's familiar. He had already returned to his spot next to Jo, and he gave me a sidelong glance as I shooed him off the stool. "There are plenty of places to sit behind the bar."

I quickly learned how it felt to get a judgmental stare from a pelican. But, when Jo added her request that Gordon move, he reluctantly flew up to the top of the wooden bar. He settled in there, looking out over the patrons. The rest of our familiars joined him, and I overheard several people comment on how cute they looked.

Valerian was hustling from one customer to the next. I was content to sit and watch her for a few minutes. It was like a dance, the way she grabbed glasses and filled them, one after another.

It was Jo who finally roused me when she asked, "What happened tonight?"

I blinked. "We did a binding spell."

"Yes, I know. But, what happened with Melba? She showed up here drunk, yelling about how she was innocent, and she just"—Jo reached up and clutched the sides of her head—"went wild."

"You did hear she was gluing Fortie's frozen peas into death-omen shapes, right?" I asked.

"Oh, of course. All of Foxfire Haven knows about that by now."

"I don't think that's what Melba was claiming to be innocent of," Marlee said. She put a hand against her heart. "What I felt from her tonight was so much stronger than someone caught in a deception. I think the constables have her at the top of their suspect list for Fortie's murder."

"If she is, then why would she come here and start throwing curses around?" Jo asked. "That seems like a strange way to prove she didn't kill him."

Marlee shrugged. "People make bad decisions when they're drunk. Melba's emotions were a mixture of sadness and frustration. She feels like someone did her wrong." Marlee shuddered, and I saw some of her dark-red magic puff out around her body.

"Hey," Jo said.

"It's just a little bit. It won't hurt anyone," Marlee countered. "I need to get Melba's emotions out of my system so I don't wind up drunk and miserable, too."

"Fair." Jo waved down Valerian. "Val, we'll take three Soothing Sodas when you get a chance. We could all use it."

"I'll pour one for myself, too!" Valerian had our sodas—which had a light vanilla flavor—in front of us just a minute later.

Facing down a desperate witch throwing curses at everyone was a good way to get the adrenaline going, and I was still feeling a bit on edge as I sipped my soda. By the time I drained the glass, though, I was feeling more relaxed. The delicious elixir really did work.

We didn't linger at the tavern long after we had finished our sodas. Several of the patrons had come over to congratulate us on our binding spell, but otherwise, the place was buzzing with speculation about what had happened to put Melba into such a state. I found the far-fetched theories tiring, and I knew Marlee was absorbing too much of everyone's curious feelings, because her shoulders kept rolling farther forward. If we didn't leave soon, she would wind up putting her head down on the bar from emotional exhaustion.

When I went to bed for the second time that night, there was no knock on my door and no one to interrupt me from turning out the light and closing my eyes. Despite how tired I was, it took a while to fall asleep. I was too busy running over my own far-fetched theories about Melba.

I woke up on Friday morning to gray skies and rain pattering softly against my window. At some point in the night, Perkins had moved from his nest to the edge of my pillow, and he was curled up in a warm ball as I yawned and stretched.

I had slept horribly.

Jo was just getting up to leave for the newspaper office as I staggered into the kitchen. She had a notebook and a pen clutched in one hand. "We're going to get some big news today!"

That helped me wake up a bit more. "How do you know?"

She tapped her pen against the notebook. "I'm manifesting it. It's been a week since Fortie was murdered, and I'm ready to have some answers. I want to write a story that's plastered on the front page of the Sunday edition, and if that's going to happen, I need to have some sensational news to write about."

I nodded toward the notebook. "You wrote what you want to happen today."

"Exactly." Jo paused, then added in a sheepish voice, "Let's hope it goes according to plan."

I winked at Jo. "Like you writing about your future room here?"

When she was looking for a new living situation, Jo had written that she wanted a laid-back place to live. When she arrived at the funeral home to see the rooms I had for rent, Jo had chosen a room that had a sloped floor. Her bed tilted on it, giving her a very different kind of "laid-back" experience than the one she'd been gunning for. The floor was slanted since the space had once been the embalming room, making it a bit of a double-backfire for Jo.

Marlee came into the kitchen long after Jo had left for work, and she didn't look like she'd slept any better than I had. She barely spoke until she had finished her first cup of coffee. When she got up to pour a second cup, she paused. "What's this?"

I turned in my chair to see what Marlee was referring to and saw her reaching between the wall and the edge of the countertop. After a moment, she pulled several photographs out of the narrow space.

"Are those more of Uncle Grant's photographs?" I asked.

"It looks like it. I saw the edge of one sticking out. Your uncle certainly took a lot of photos."

"And stashed them all over the place. I keep stumbling across them, too."

"It's like a scavenger hunt. How fun." Marlee refilled her coffee cup, then brought it and the photos over to the kitchen table. "Let's take a look."

Uncle Grant was older in the one photo he appeared in, which meant it hadn't been taken that many years before his death. Another was of the funeral home, and the third was a nature scene. "I guess he was an amateur photographer," I said as I appreciated a shot of fir trees wreathed in fog. "I never knew."

"Hazel," Marlee said slowly. When I looked at her, she laid the photo in her hand on the table, so we could both see it. "Tell me what you see in this shot."

"That's the showroom," I said immediately. "Better known as our living room." There was a line of caskets, all different colors, ranging from basic to garishly ornate. They were neatly lined up along one of the walls. "I don't know who that man is, though. Maybe he worked for my uncle."

"Take a closer look at him," Marlee insisted.

I leaned down toward the photo. At a glance, he had simply looked like a man with dark hair and a thick beard, and he was wearing a dark suit. He was standing behind one of the caskets, so he was only visible from the waist up.

As I took a closer look, though, I realized I could see the pattern of the floral wallpaper overlaid on the man's form. *No,* I realized. *I'm seeing the wallpaper through the man.*

I sat up straight with a gasp. "He's not a solid form. Is this a ghost?"

"It's definitely not Holman."

"But if there is another ghost here, then Holman would know about it."

Marlee grinned. "Which means we need to summon him, and I know exactly how to do it. Be right back!" Marlee scooted out of the kitchen, and even though I knew she was going to return wearing something ugly enough to get Holman's attention, I still burst out laughing when she reappeared. She had donned a pair of plum-colored trousers and a fluorescent-green T-shirt. To top it all off, Marlee had added a blue plastic lei.

"I knew I'd kept this for a reason," Marlee said, giving the lei a gentle tug. "One of my clients had a luau for their wedding reception."

"Ouch! My eyes!" Holman had wasted no time, showing up to comment on Marlee's ensemble.

"I guess you didn't have clothing this bright back in your day," Marlee said cheerfully. "You can thank the nineteen eighties for this shirt. I found it at a thrift store and couldn't resist."

Holman crossed his arms and tilted his body, giving the appearance of leaning against the doorframe. Of course, as a ghost, he would slide right through it if he tilted any farther. "You have good taste, as I said before.

I know you put this outfit on because you wanted to get my attention. Please, tell me what you want quickly, so I can go away and stop looking at this abomination."

Marlee strode to the kitchen table and pointed at the photo. "We just want to know who this is."

Holman shrugged. "I don't know, but he could sure use a beard trim."

"Look closer," I instructed, just as Marlee had told me to do.

Holman sucked in a breath as he realized the man was transparent. "Oh. Oh, dear."

"We were surprised, too," I said. "It appears there's another ghost haunting the funeral home."

CHAPTER TWENTY-FIVE

MARLEE GLANCED OVER HER shoulder, then let her eyes trail across the space above her head. "I'm okay with Holman, but I'm not sure I like the idea of another ghost running around this place."

"Who is he, anyway? And did Uncle Grant realize he captured a ghost on film?" I wondered.

"It's not someone I recall ever seeing, living or otherwise," Holman said. "Whoever he is, don't assume he's still here. I haven't met anyone haunting this place. This ghost might have made a temporary stay here during my banishment."

"And, maybe, the ghost moved to a new home once you came back." I paused, then added, "Or Grant banished him, too."

Uncle Grant had been so paranoid in his final years that he had temporarily banished Holman, so the ghost couldn't see what Grant was up to in his fanatical search for some mysterious object. Or hidden treasure. It all depended on which Foxfire Haven old-timer's story one wanted to believe.

"Or the ghost is still here, and he's the one who likes to leave the front door wide open," Marlee suggested. She was still looking around the kitchen anxiously.

Holman made a noise of disdain. "If that's all he can do, then I don't think any of us need to worry about him."

That seemed to calm Marlee a bit. She settled into her chair at the table, then thanked Holman for his help.

"Sure. But, the next time you need me, please put on something a bit less atrocious. You don't need to work this hard to get my attention." Holman quickly faded.

"Do you think he's jealous?" Marlee asked in a whisper.

"Who?" I realized I was also whispering. "Are we trying not to be overheard by a ghost?"

Marlee laughed self-consciously, and when she spoke again, her voice was at its normal volume. "Yeah, but if Holman is still here, I guess he can stand close and hear every word I say without me knowing, anyway. I wonder if he's jealous that this other ghost can open the door. Holman can't manipulate physical objects, right?"

"Right. But, like Holman said, we don't know if this other ghost is the one opening the front door. The two things might not be related."

"That would leave us with two mysteries to solve: who this bearded ghost is, and how is the front door is opening by itself."

"I'd be satisfied to solve just one mystery, and that's who killed Fortie." I shook my head as I gestured toward the photo of the ghost. "His murder is like this photo. I can almost see the whole picture, but not quite. Something's missing."

My conversation with Wyatt came rushing back to me. *I haven't found the one thread that ties all the others together.*

Then, the thing I'd been saying for the past week came to mind, as well. "But, of course, I'm not trying to solve this murder."

Marlee remained silent, but her skeptical look spoke volumes.

I had two deliveries to make that day, and when I left for the first one, Marlee was at work in the dining room. She had covered the table in white organza bags, which she was stuffing with a combination of crystals, flower seeds, and small vials of bubbles. Perkins, Stella, and Lonnie were lined up on the perch we'd built from a giant fallen tree branch. Gordon, I assumed, was out fishing.

It was two o'clock in the afternoon by the time I'd wrapped up my deliveries, and my stomach was loudly complaining that I hadn't stopped for lunch yet. "Soon," I promised. "Just one more stop."

That one stop was the constable station. I wanted to check on Melba, and I didn't want to risk calling and talking to anyone who might give a vague answer. Instead, I was going straight to the chief constable.

The constable sitting at the desk just inside the front door of the station gave me a brief smile when I walked inside. "Hello. How can I help you?"

"I'm here to see Wy—Chief Constable Hightower, please."

The man narrowed his eyes. "What's your name and business?"

"Hazel Underwood. I'm here to follow up on someone who was brought in last night."

"The witch." I wasn't sure if the constable was referring to Melba or me. "The Chief Constable is a very busy man. I can give you an update, though."

"I was one of the people she tried to curse," I pointed out. "In fact, she tried to curse my entire coven."

The constable's eyebrows lifted slowly. "You're one of the ladies who brought her down. Sure, head on back. His office is the second door on your right."

I felt a lightness in my step as I headed down the hallway toward Wyatt's office. The look of respect the constable had given me after realizing who I was had made me feel good. For once, my magic had made someone appreciate me. It was a far cry from the shame of my magical exhalations.

Wyatt's door was open, so I rapped my knuckles against it lightly before walking through the doorway.

"Oh, Underwood. Come in." Wyatt looked haggard, like he hadn't slept well, either. "Do you have news for me?"

"No, but Jo says there's going to be some big news related to Fortie today." When Wyatt gave me a skeptical look, I added, "She's manifesting it."

"Great. Let's just solve all crimes with magic. Then I can retire."

He was in a bad mood. Not that I'd ever seen Wyatt in a good mood. He was just extra-surly.

"We still need you and the constables," I assured him. "And, like I said, no, I don't have news. I came to check on Melba. She was in a bad state last night, and I wanted to make sure she's going to be okay."

Wyatt looked out the window of his office, which afforded a view of a sweet little tree-lined street. "We held her overnight. She had quite the hangover this morning."

"But you let her go?"

"Yes. She has to pay a fine and take a magical ethics course before she can have her business license reinstated, and she's got a lot of community service hours to get through."

"I'm glad it's not worse than that. She was so upset last night."

"We brought her in for questioning after you sent Newton over here to tell us she was the one who had faked the death omens. She didn't deal with it very well, but she'll come through this just fine." Wyatt's eyes were teasing as he added, "It was very kind of you to check on her."

"I never did finish that kindness spell. Look at that! I can be kind without magic."

"I knew you had it in you."

When I walked out of Wyatt's office, I felt like I had left him in a better mood than he'd been in when I had arrived. It was a small victory, but one that gave me a lot of satisfaction.

No sooner had I climbed behind the wheel of the hearse again than my phone rang. It was Jo, and she sounded excited as she said, "Where are you? How soon can you get to the tavern? And is Marlee with you?"

"Constable station, two minutes, no. What's going on?"

"I'll explain there. See you soon." Jo hung up without another word, presumably to call Marlee and ask her the same rapid-fire questions.

Jo might have gotten the news she was hoping to manifest, so I quickly started up the engine and headed for the tavern rather than home. I'd enjoy chicken fingers and fries more than a sandwich and chips, anyway.

The tavern was mostly empty, since it was the middle of the afternoon. Even Barry was absent as I hopped up onto a stool right in the middle of the long bar. "Before Jo gets here," I told Valerian, "I need to order lunch. I'm starving."

Valerian put my order in right before Jo burst through the door. She tossed her braids over her shoulder as she hurried toward me. "Marlee said she'd be here."

"I take it your manifesting has produced some results," I commented.

"Maybe. We have a possible new suspect, at any rate." Jo looked over her shoulder. "Where is she? I want to tell all of you at once."

Jo was so wound up she wouldn't even sit. She paced back and forth behind my barstool until Valerian told her she was making the few other patrons nervous. That got Jo to stand still, but since she couldn't work off her energy with walking, she resorted to tapping her fingers against the nearest barstool, instead.

Luckily, Marlee came in just a minute later, before the noise of Jo's fingers against the vinyl cover on the barstool could really get to me.

Marlee sat on the stool to my left while Valerian leaned over the bar. The three of us looked at Jo expectantly.

"Someone showed up at city hall this morning," Jo began. "An outsider who said he had a deal with Fortie, and he'd been trying to find out who his new contact would be. The man said the answer he got at Fortie's office building led nowhere. So, today, the clerk at city hall explained Fortie was a one-man operation, and the outsider said there must be someone who was taking over his business affairs."

"Let me guess," I cut in. "He's from Stanton, and he had worked up a proposal for Fortie."

Jo gaped at me. "How did you know?"

I briefly described my encounter with the businessman when I had been loading the last things from Fortie's office. Then, I added, "But I don't see how he's a suspect. The guy was trying to do business with Fortie, not kill him."

"That's just it," Jo said excitedly. "When the clerk said there was no one handling Fortie's business dealings, since his business had just been him, the man from Stanton said that, maybe, he could cut out the middleman entirely."

"It seems like a stretch to go from shrewd businessman to murder suspect," Marlee said.

Jo looked crestfallen. "I know. But I wrote that manifestation intention this morning, and here it is, almost three o'clock, and it hasn't worked yet. I guess I'm seeing a connection where there is none."

"Who was the man, anyway?" I asked. "He never did introduce himself to me."

"Oh, I wrote it down somewhere. Peterson, I think. Paul Peterson."

Valerian's mouth formed an *O*. "That's not just a person. It's a business. My ex brother-in-law did some work for him in Stanton. Paul Peterson Contracting is the biggest construction company in that town."

"The question, then," I said, "is what was Fortie hoping to build, and did it get him killed?"

CHAPTER TWENTY-SIX

"YOU SHOULD TELL WYATT," I added immediately.

"I said the same thing to the clerk who told me the story," Jo said. "I'm sure the constables are already following up on the lead."

"Fortie lived in the old Harper mansion on the west side of town," Marlee told us. "I wonder if he was going to renovate the place. It's been falling apart for years."

"But why would someone kill him over that?" Valerian wondered.

"I expect Hazel is right," Jo said, still sounding disappointed. "Paul Peterson—the man and his business—probably have nothing to do with Fortie's murder. He just has bad timing."

A bell dinged behind Valerian, and she turned to retrieve my lunch order from the small window that separated the bar area from the kitchen in the back. I eagerly began eating as soon as the plate was in front of me.

"Someone worked up an appetite while looking for clues," Marlee teased.

"I was doing no such thing," I said after downing a fry. "I had two deliveries today, and then I stopped at the constable station to get an update on Melba."

"I heard she's got a wicked hangover today," Valerian said.

I relayed what Wyatt had told me about Melba's situation, and they all agreed she might come back stronger and better than ever. "People will feel sorry for her now, so they'll really want to give her their business," Marlee speculated.

Valerian looked past us in the direction of the door. "People should feel sorry for me. My most finicky patron just walked in."

The rest of us turned and saw Euphoria and Newton walking toward the bar. "Which one do you mean?" I asked.

Valerian didn't need to answer, because Euphoria called out, "A dirty martini. Extra dirty, extra olives. And by extra, I don't mean two, like the last time."

As Valerian got to work, Newton came over to the rest of us, his usual fake-looking smile plastered on his face. "Hello, ladies. I seem to run into you everywhere I go! May I buy you a round of drinks?"

All three of us thanked Newton for the offer but turned him down. Jo and Marlee both said they had to get back to work, and I was heading to the magic store as soon as I finished my lunch.

Newton seemed undaunted. "Mayor Lachlan, aren't these ladies just what we love about Foxfire Haven? I hear this coven helped the constables arrest Melba Hawthorn last night."

Euphoria turned to us with a sneer, but after a glance at Newton, she pulled her lips into a shape that was almost a smile. "It's nice to know the local witches are supporting our law enforcement." Euphoria seemed to think she had contributed enough, or maybe it was all she could muster of politeness, because she quickly turned away to watch Valerian closely.

When Valerian put the martini glass down in front of Euphoria, at least a dozen olives were piled inside it.

Newton and Euphoria moved off to sit at one of the booths, and I was able to finish my lunch in peace. I wished my coven a good afternoon once I'd paid, then headed out for Into the Cauldron.

Foxfire Haven's magic store wasn't far from the tavern, so it was an easy walk. Really, anything in downtown was an easy walk. Magical towns were usually very small. That meant it didn't take long to get anywhere.

It also meant I was more likely to run into people I knew whenever I went somewhere. When I walked through the door of Into the Cauldron, the first person I saw was Melba Hawthorn. She looked so hungover it made my own head ache a little, and I wondered if some of Marlee's empath magic was rubbing off on me.

No, I told myself. *She takes on the emotions of others, not their physical pain.* Melba was radiating so much misery it was palpable.

Melba turned when she heard the door opening, and I hoped she wouldn't recognize me. She had been so drunk the night before that I didn't know if she had even registered the witches who performed the binding spell on her.

When Melba returned her attention to a display of mugwort, I relaxed. Soon, I was working through my own magical shopping list.

I had just stepped up to the counter to pay when I heard a quiet, "Excuse me." I turned to see Melba standing there. Her face was sallow, and she was squinting slightly, like the overhead lights hurt her eyes.

"You're part of the funeral home coven," she said.

I nodded. That was one way of identifying us, I supposed.

"I'm sorry I tried to curse you. The four of you did the right thing by binding my magic. If you hadn't stopped me, I might have hurt someone."

"We're happy it all got resolved before something bad could happen."

Melba lifted the small basket she was carrying in one hand. It was stuffed with herbs, candles, and a few vials of different-colored liquids. "As soon as this hangover fades, I'm going to do a Reset Your Reputation spell. Though, I must say, being scandalous has proven to be good for business."

"I tried to book a consultation with you on your website this week, but there were no free openings. I'm sure it helps to be so busy, now that you don't have money from Fortie coming in."

"It does help. I'll miss taking that man's money, though."

There was something about Melba's tone that caught my attention. Clearly, it wasn't just the income she was going to miss, but taking it from Fortie himself. "You were helping him, but it sounds like you didn't care for him."

Melba shrugged. "I'm never going to like all of my clients." She paused, and I thought that was all the information I was going to get. With a little sigh, though, Melba added, "Yes, I enjoyed making Fortie think he was going to die, then taking more and more of his money to help him stay alive. The more I took from him, the less he could save up for his awful plan."

"You make him sound downright diabolical."

The teenager working the cash register gave me the total for my purchase, and I absently handed over my credit card. I was too absorbed in what Melba was saying to pay attention to how much I was spending.

"I love this town," Melba said. "Where else can I buy plants from a gnome, then run into a Bigfoot while on my morning walk through the woods? Fortie, though, he fell out of love with Foxfire Haven a long time ago. He cared more about power and money."

"I did hear he liked pushing around local business owners, using his position on the city council to get what he wanted."

"It wasn't just that." Melba's fingers tightened around the handle of the basket. "He was going to buy the land next to my house. He was saving up for it, but the more I took from him, the more likely it was that I'd be able to buy the land before he could."

What Gemma had told us was true, then. Melba had forested land next to her house, and she didn't want anyone else getting their hands on it. Had Melba killed Fortie over a tract of land?

"Fortie recently got a proposal from a contractor in Stanton," I said, nodding. "We were wondering why, but it sounds like he had plans for that land, even though he hadn't bought it yet."

Melba grimaced. "He was going to open a franchise for a burger chain. Fortie thought he'd make a mint by catering to people driving down the highway. Think of all the outside people that would bring in! Even though the land is on the edge of town, that's still too close for non-magical people to be getting to Foxfire Haven. Lots of people in town wouldn't have wanted Fortie to follow through with his plan."

I knew Melba was right. If word had started getting around that Fortie was going to bring in a lot of road-trippers from the highway with his fast-food restaurant plan, then plenty of people would be upset about it.

There was one person, I realized, who had even more reason to object.

"Thank you, Melba," I said breathlessly.

"For what? For apologizing to you? It was the least I could do."

"No. For helping me figure out who killed Fortie."

CHAPTER TWENTY-SEVEN

MELBA'S EYES OPENED FULLY, her hangover forgotten in her surprise. "What? I don't know who killed him."

"No, but what you said just now made me realize who had the best motive. I have to get to the constable station." I thanked Melba again, and I was already walking toward the front door when the clerk hollered that I had forgotten my purchase. I hurried back over, grabbed my bag, then left both the clerk and Melba standing in shocked silence.

I practically ran out the front door because I was so anxious to talk to Wyatt. Unfortunately, I ran right into Euphoria. "Oh, sorry!" I said, stepping back.

Before I could move around her, Euphoria pointed a finger at me, her manicured fingernail just inches from my face. "Don't you dare do it," she hissed.

My eyebrows drew down. "Do what?"

"Tell Chief Constable Hightower that I killed Fortie."

I gaped at Euphoria. I had shocked Melba by declaring I knew who had killed Fortie, and now, it was my turn to be caught off guard. My mouth moved, but no words came out because I didn't know how to respond. Eventually, I stammered, "Why would I tell him that?"

"I overheard your coven at the tavern. They were talking about the murder after you left, and the reporter mentioned a contractor from Stanton who was planning something with Fortie." Euphoria finally dropped her hand so she could cross her arms. "You know how I feel about protecting this town. About keeping outside people away."

Euphoria glared at me in a way that said she considered me to be one of those outside people, since I had lived in the non-magical world for so long. "I didn't know that for sure," I said. "After all, I did hear you hired an outside wedding planner."

Euphoria opened her mouth to retort, but I cut her off. "Since you're backing Newton, though, and he's mentioned his feelings about Foxfire Haven, I did assume that you two have similar views."

"So, you also assume I killed Fortie to protect my town."

As I shook my head, I spotted a group of people hurrying along the sidewalk toward us. Jo, Marlee, and Valerian were trailing in Wyatt's wake. Gordon, Stella, and Lonnie were flying low circles around the group, all squawking loudly.

"What are you all doing here?" I asked as the foursome reached us. I was happy to see my coven, but Euphoria looked annoyed by their appearance.

"Euphoria stalked out of the tavern," Jo said, "and a few minutes later, Gordon swooped through the front door. I knew something was wrong, and our best guess was that Euphoria was going after you for some reason." Jo gave Euphoria a cool look. "I see we were correct."

"And the toucan and the raven came to get me," Wyatt said. "They flew into my office and made a racket until I promised to follow them."

I looked at the three birds, who had settled on top of a nearby bench and fallen silent as they watched us closely. "Where's Perkins?"

"Watching over you, of course," Valerian said. She nodded toward the window of Into the Cauldron, and I saw Perkins sitting on the sill. He looked very proud of himself. "Our familiars have been keeping a close watch on us since the incident with Melba last night." Valerian's gaze shifted to a spot behind me. "Hello, Melba."

Melba had come out of the store at some point, and when I glanced over my shoulder, I saw she was watching the scene with rapt attention. She gave Valerian the barest of nods, too absorbed in what was going on to pay heed to the fact that our familiars were trying to guard us from her.

"Chief Constable, don't believe a word this woman says," Euphoria said sharply. "She hates me, and she's determined to slander my name. I did not kill Fortie Fortenbacher."

I heaved a long-suffering sigh. "Euphoria, if you had let me get a word in edgewise, I would have told you that I don't think you killed Fortie."

Melba stepped forward. "Then who did? You told me that you'd figured it out."

"Of course she did," Wyatt muttered.

"Wyatt, I know this is going to sound like a stretch," I warned.

Before I could continue, our familiars began making a racket. Perkins lifted into the air and fluttered to my shoulder. Jo, Marlee, and Valerian all turned to look in the same direction as the birds, and I spotted Newton and Julian walking toward us.

If this kept up, half of Foxfire Haven would be hanging out on the sidewalk in front of the magic store.

Newton began to laugh as he sidled between Wyatt and Marlee. "My favorite witches, we meet again!"

Wyatt took half a step toward me. "Come on, Hazel, let's discuss this at the station."

I shook my head. "No need. You can ask Julian right now if he killed Fortie."

Euphoria laughed incredulously. "Oh, please."

Julian, though, wasn't laughing. His expression froze as he stared, tight-lipped, at me.

"And what proof do you have for that accusation?" Wyatt asked. His voice was stern, but I thought I also detected a note of pride.

"I don't have proof. But Fortie was planning to franchise a burger place. He was going to buy some vacant land that's for sale between here and the highway. Like Melba said to me a few minutes ago, people in Foxfire Haven would be upset about a chain fast-food restaurant coming in and attracting non-magical people. But you know who would be even more concerned? Someone who owns the only burger restaurant in town. Valerian mentioned Julian runs Foxfire Grill."

Julian didn't so much as blink, but Euphoria choked out another laugh. "You think Julian killed Fortie because he didn't want competition for his restaurant?"

"Yes," I said without hesitation.

To my surprise, Melba was the one who jumped in to support me. "It makes sense. Fortie told Newton about his plan, and Newton blabbed about it to Julian. Of course, Julian was furious about it, and he confronted Fortie. Julian told him it would drive a magical mom-and-pop place out of business."

"And how do you know about that?" Wyatt asked, turning his attention to Melba.

She shrugged. "Fortie told me lots of things."

"She's right." Newton's voice was so low I had to lean forward to hear him. "Oh, this is awful. If I hadn't told Julian, then maybe Fortie would still be alive. It's my fault he's dead."

"Oh, hogwash," Valerian snapped. "The only person to blame for Fortie's death is the killer. If you didn't inject him with that extract of deadly nightshade, then it's not your fault."

Newton's eyes were beginning to bulge, but Valerian was already moving to take his hand. On his other side, Marlee was gripping his forearm.

We were all watching Newton when Julian began to run. He elbowed his way past Euphoria and me, his leather loafers pelting against the sidewalk.

Julian was quick, but our familiars were quicker. All four of them took flight. Gordon and Lonnie zoomed in front of Julian while Stella and Perkins followed. The distraction was enough to slow Julian down, and Wyatt was a blur as he shot past me and tackled Julian.

As Wyatt climbed off Julian and the two men stood, I only understood pieces of what Julian was shouting. His face was red as he said things about greed, hamburgers, and his family legacy. Wyatt let him yell while he pulled a set of handcuffs off his belt.

Wyatt called for a squad car, and by the time one rolled up to the curb five minutes later, Julian had stopped shouting. He still looked defiant, though.

Euphoria had snuck away at some point, probably worried her friendship with Julian would somehow implicate her in the murder. I wasn't worried about her, though. Julian, I was certain, had acted alone.

Wyatt got Julian into the back of the squad car, then came over to me. "I'll call you later about giving a statement. For now, though, thank you."

"I'm glad I could help," I said honestly.

After Wyatt had left in the squad car, Melba turned to Jo, Marlee, and Valerian. She repeated the apology she had given me, then asked if there was anything she could do to make up for having tried to curse us.

"Give us a free consultation with you," Marlee suggested. "Hazel has been trying to book with you, and I think it would be fun to have another coven outing."

"Absolutely!" Melba smiled, then put a hand to her head. "Ouch. I'll get in touch about a day and time. Right now, I need to go home and get a Hangover Helper spell started."

Once Melba had disappeared around the corner, Jo grinned. "I'm going to have a busy evening, but it will feel awfully good to see my story on the front page of the Sunday edition."

"Come by the tavern for dinner later," Valerian said. "I'm working a double tonight."

"I will, but I won't be ordering a burger." Jo made a face of mock disgust.

Gordon squawked out a noise that sounded like a laugh. He, Lonnie, and Stella were on the bench again, and Perkins had joined them.

"We got this taken care of faster because of all of you," Marlee told our familiars. "Thank you for being such a big help."

"Yes," I added. "It was very kind of you."

CHAPTER TWENTY-EIGHT

JAZZ WAS LYING ON his side in the grass, right at the edge of the funeral home's lawn.

"I think he's trying to make peace with the birds," Jo noted. She lifted her mug and took a sip of her steaming tea. "He wants to prove he's safe to be around."

"I have to leave in an hour for a cake-tasting appointment," Marlee said. "I expect one of you to text me if there's any familiar drama this evening."

Valerian pulled her cardigan tighter around her body. "It beats murder drama."

We were sitting on the front porch, enjoying a rare sunny day. It wasn't warm outside by any means, but it wasn't freezing cold, either. It had been two days since Wyatt had arrested Julian for Fortie's murder, and a lazy Sunday afternoon on the porch felt like the perfect way to reward ourselves.

Jo was also celebrating her front-page news story.

"There are two open spots on the city council now," Valerian continued. "I'm a little disappointed I have today off, because I bet the gossip at the tavern is great."

"You should run for one of the spots, Haze," Marlee said with a laugh. "Then you could see Euphoria all the time!"

"No, thank you! Besides, I don't have time to be a politician. I have my hands full fixing up this place, running the delivery service, and working with Hailey."

"But you've got us to help with that last one," Jo pointed out.

After seeing how powerful we were against Melba, we had decided to do a group spell for my granddaughter. It was a simple one designed to help Hailey control her magic.

"Speaking of which," I said, looking at my watch, "we should go get ready for that."

Soon, we were sitting on one side of the dining room table, our chairs as close as they could be so Hailey would be able to see all four of us on her screen. In front of us, we had a bundle of dried sage, a candle, and a large onyx.

Tara looked wary when she initiated the video call. When I had told her about our idea, she had looked uncomfortable, and I had half-expected her to turn down the offer. She had reluctantly agreed, but I could see she still had her doubts.

Hailey, on the other hand, looked excited when her face popped up on the screen. "Witches!" she declared as she gazed at us.

"That's right," I told her. "And we're good witches who use our magic to do good things."

"Like catch bad people," Marlee added.

"And, today, we're going to do good magic for you." Jo was beaming at Hailey.

Valerian would be leading us, as usual, and she lifted the onyx, holding it close to the screen so Hailey could see it clearly. "This will help you control your magic. Are you ready to start the magic spell?"

"Ready!" Hailey narrowed her eyes and pursed her lips, which was the face she made when she was concentrating on something.

Valerian put the crystal down so she could light the candle, and then she held the sage bundle over it. Once the sage was smoking, she blew out the flame and waved the bundle in a circle around the onyx. She calmly and clearly began to chant the simple words to the spell, which would be easy enough for Hailey to learn.

Halfway through the second recitation, Hailey suddenly giggled, and the screen went black. Valerian abruptly cut off reciting the incantation while Jo and Marlee gasped.

"Well," I quipped, "at least she's going to be a powerful witch."

A NOTE FROM THE AUTHOR

I had so much fun writing this book! I knew I wanted to have a character who divined the future using some unusual method, and I giggled when I pictured a bag of frozen peas being ripped open and their contents examined. I hope it gave you a laugh, too. As usual, I appreciate you being here with me on this adventure.

Will you please leave a review before you go? It helps spread the word for other paranormal cozy fans.

Eternally Yours,

Beth

P.S. You can keep up with my latest book news, get fun freebies, and more by signing up for my newsletter at BethDolgner.com!

Next in Series

Find out what's next for Hazel and the Crones of a Feather!

Manifesting and Mischief
Crones of a Feather Paranormal Cozy Mysteries Book 3

A bossy witch, a bag full of cash, and supernatural allies. Can words really be deadly?

Wintertime in Foxfire Haven heats up with the arrival of a brash witch intent on buying the town newspaper. At the same time, other newcomers to the magical town are raising eyebrows everywhere they go.

When the witch winds up dead, Hazel Underwood is determined to solve the murder. After all, a member of her own coven is one of the suspects. Did Jo kill just to protect her career with the newspaper?

As she tracks down clues, Hazel must rely on the teamwork of her coven for everything from spells for a good outcome to warding off increasing paranormal activity at the former funeral home where they live. And will Hazel and Chief Constable Wyatt Hightower ever find a way to work together?

Acknowledgments

Whenever I finish a manuscript, there's always a little part of me that worries. *Is it any good? Have I gotten too ridiculous this time, writing about things like frozen peas that tell the future?* My test readers are always there to tell me what's working and what isn't. I owe a big thank-you to them—Kristine, Sabrina, Alex, David, Lisa, and Mom. My street team and ARC readers helped launch this series with a lot of fanfare, and I'm grateful for their continued help. My editors, Lia at Your Best Book Editor and Trish at Blossoming Pages, always help me produce as professional of a book as possible.

BOOKS BY BETH DOLGNER

Crones of a Feather
Paranormal Cozy Mystery Series
Spells and Subterfuge
Divination and Deceit
Manifesting and Mischief

Nightmare, Arizona
Paranormal Cozy Mystery Series
Homicide at the Haunted House
Drowning at the Diner
Slaying at the Saloon
Murder at the Motel
Poisoning at the Party
Headless at Halloween (Novella)
Clawing at the Corral
Axing at the Antique Store
Fatality at the Festival
Terminated at the Trailhead
Body at the Bakery

Eternal Rest Bed and Breakfast
Paranormal Cozy Mystery Series

Sweet Dreams
Late Checkout
Picture Perfect
Destination Wedding (Novella)
Scenic Views
Breakfast Included
Groups Welcome
Quiet Nights
Halloween Vibes (Novella)

Betty Boo, Ghost Hunter
Romantic Urban Fantasy Series
Ghost of a Threat
Ghost of a Whisper
Ghost of a Memory
Ghost of a Hope

Manifest
Young Adult Steampunk

A Talent for Death
Young Adult Urban Fantasy

Non-fiction
Georgia Spirits and Specters
Everyday Voodoo

ABOUT THE AUTHOR

Beth Dolgner's career as an author began in nonfiction with *Georgia Spirits and Specters*, a collection of Georgia ghost stories. From there, Beth entered the world of ghost hunting and was a longtime guide with the Roswell Ghost Tour in Georgia. She also lectures on Victorian death and mourning customs as well as Victorian Spiritualism, which stemmed from her volunteer work with Atlanta's Historic Oakland Cemetery. Beth likes to think of it all as research for her books.

Outside of writing, Beth enjoys traveling, sewing, and trying to convince her husband, Ed, that ghosts are real.

Keep up with Beth and sign up for her newsletter at BethDolgner.com.

www.ingramcontent.com/pod-product-compliance
Lightning Source LLC
Chambersburg PA
CBHW020103180626
46812CB00006B/2447